# *The*
# *Perpetual Order*
# *Of Old People*

A novel by

Jeff Russell

**Cabern
Publishing**

*The Perpetual Order of Old People* is a work of fiction, except for those parts that are inspired by some true-life unsung heroes who meet for coffee every morning and have graciously shared their stories with me so that I may share them with you. Otherwise, all names, characters, places, and incidents are the product of the author's imagination or are used fictitiously. Any resemblance to actual businesses, organizations, events, locales or persons, living or dead, is entirely coincidental.

ISBN-13   978-0-9895421-6-6

This work is dedicated to an older generation that blazed a trail and set an example for the rest of us to follow. My deepest thanks to Will, John, Vic, Don, and Mac … real people with real stories they have shared to make this book possible. May those stories always be told and cherished.

And a special thanks to my wife, Mary, who understands that my passion for writing justifies the countless hours I spend hunched over a keyboard. This is a story about lives shared and I am so fortunate to be sharing mine with you.

Finally, a big thanks to Mu for teaching me to speak in Crow. May your feathers always shine.

# The Perpetual Order of Old People

## Chapter 1

### *January 2007*

She called me an old fool, a misanthrope, an egotistic recluse who shunned affection, feared commitment and was destined to die lonely and miserable. That is only partially true.

I have always felt the need to be an integral part of something greater than myself. For half a century I advanced from one responsibility to the next while seeking to make a significant contribution, to be the foundation upon which others built, the compass providing direction and the mainspring that kept things running. Leading men, formulating strategy, executing plans and achieving results fed my spirit the way air feeds lungs. Success was as vital as breathing; failure as painful as suffocation. Simply put, the goal in every aspect of my career was to serve an essential role in some noble purpose.

And I have always enjoyed working with others. During my tour in the military, I had a superb personal relationship with the officers and enlisted under my command. A shared sense of duty binds men as brothers and, in that respect, I was a part of their family and they a part of mine, a privilege that lasted twenty proud years. Even after resigning my commission and going into business for myself, wheeling and dealing with power brokers day and night, dining with them, meeting their spouses, listening to stories of their children, I felt accepted into their fold. We were a clan, complete with the rivalries, bickering, support, and celebration that all families cherish.

Retirement changed everything. I hadn't anticipated venturing into this next phase of my life without the noble purpose or surrogate families that had always been there for me. My existence has become inconsequential, with no new challenges to propel me out of bed in the morning and no congratulations for a job well done. Days that were never long enough now drag on interminably and nights are spent wondering what went wrong. I have come to accept that freedom is not enough, that past accomplishment cannot fill the lungs with anticipation and possessions cannot quiet the voice inside that craves the sound of another's voice. When the questions and isolation and boredom become too much I seek the peace and distraction of a long, contemplative walk.

Walking is my elixir, my fountain of youth, the ideal blend of physically demanding and mentally therapeutic. I prefer to walk outdoors, early and aggressively, burning calories, recharging my psyche and taking in nature's glory. On a day like today, however, when the fickle and often harsh New England weather refuses to cooperate I head for the local shopping mall. At its worst, which is to say during the holiday season, when the concourse is crammed, the commotion is deafening, tempers are short and lines are long and moving about means colliding with someone, it is then that the mall holds its greatest allure. I believe it relates back to being around people at a time when friends and family come together, to fond memories of siblings and relatives sitting shoulder-to-shoulder at the dinner table, arms reaching this way and that for a shaker of salt or basket of rolls, everyone talking at once and happy to be there. Those were good times, carefree, intimate times and it is worth being inadvertently bumped for a chance to experience that feeling again.

And at its best, when the shopping is over and the crowds are gone the mall still retains its magnetic charm. There is peace in its passages, a quiet that allows one to appreciate the music in the background and a place to walk undisturbed and unconcerned, free of the woes of traffic and weather. Being there offers an opportunity to relax and recuperate, tranquility akin to sitting by the fireplace and watching the embers glow after the guests have gone home.

It is actually a very stylish mall, as indoor malls go. Expansive yet intimate, commercial yet comfortable. Glass panels form a cathedral ceiling that runs the length of the main concourse, bathing the interior with sunlight during the day and offering a canopy of stars at night. A majestic fountain serves as the centerpiece of the lower level while the upper level is designed as a wrap-around balcony, open in the center to provide patrons with a clear view of everything the mall has to offer. Shopping opportunities range from major retailers to startups, anchor stores to kiosks, name brands to unknowns hoping to become the next big thing. Avenues jutting off the main on both levels provide access to additional stores and effectively double the distance I can walk without retracing my steps. The architecture is modern with spacious views and warm colors throughout. Soft lighting from decorative fabric globes falls on wood trimmed pillars and handrails, and oak benches placed here and there invite shoppers to sit and unwind.

My goal is to arrive before the stores open for business, though even then the mall is a beehive of activity with managers setting up shop, workers finishing some overnight task and maintenance crews getting things tidy. And there are always other walkers present, everyone from speed-demons to couples strolling hand-in-hand. Yet minus the throngs of shoppers, I can set my own course and pace, relishing a chance to be alone without actually being alone. The typical routine is two loops of the lower level, then a coffee break, followed by two loops of the top. That was the plan for today but as I picked up my decaf in the food court I heard what sounded like an invitation.

"Have a seat, sailor."

I didn't know him, the older fellow with the thinning grey hair and outgoing smile, but I'd seen him there on numerous occasions over the past year, sitting with friends around two long tables pushed together. I would nod if one of them looked up as I passed by and invariably someone would return the gesture and smile.

# The Perpetual Order of Old People

Such is the nature of gentlemen, and despite their jesting and the aura of bravado, they were clearly gentlemen. I arrived earlier than normal this morning and found him sitting alone.

"Come on," he said. "Tie-up alongside." He used his cane to pull a chair from a nearby table and positioned it next to his. "What sub?" he asked.

It took a moment to make the connection ... the dolphin insignia on my belt buckle. That buckle, still clamped to the same web belt I wore back then is the last memento of my days in the submarine service. I've worn that belt practically every day since, putting it on each morning without thinking. It is part of my ensemble, much as my father's Marine Corps ring was part of his. He wore that ring from the day he left the service to the day he died ... and then some.

"Have a seat," my host said again.

Instinct told me to keep going. He was part of a group, possibly part of a larger group, and I have always steered clear of civic organizations – formal or otherwise. I respect and appreciate the role they play but marching in parades, soliciting donations and paying dues for the pleasure of companionship never appealed to me. Yet as I hesitated I began to thaw, wondering if he had also been part of the 'silent service', and despite my reservations, I complied.

He reached out his hand. "Tom Johnson, USS Blueback, SS 581." There was authority in his handshake, a sense of pride that I seldom encounter in the civilian world, and I did my best to reciprocate.

"Jack Brouder, USS George Washington, SSBN 598."

"Boomer, huh? Didn't they do something with her, a museum or something?"

The conversation had been buried inside me for too long, aching to be heard and waiting for the appropriate audience. This was my chance. "Part of her. They scrapped the boat but kept the sail. It's mounted at the entrance to the Sub Force Museum in Groton, across from the Nautilus and just outside the main gate of the Sub Base."

My thoughts drifted as I recalled the sail, what some might call the conning tower, as it exists today. Tall, shiny and black, with the planes stretched out like wings and the hull number painted on the side. A Polaris missile stands in the background, the same type of missile we carried on patrol forty-some years earlier.

"I've been up to see it a few times," I continued. "It looks smaller than I remember, probably because they cut it off level with the missile deck rather than the forward hull, but it's still impressive."

"That's right," Tom noted. "I remember seeing something online about it. Nice tribute. They kept the Blueback intact. Now she's tied-up and serves as a museum piece in Portland. Nice that they do that, and they should do it. Blueback was the last of the diesel-electrics, Nautilus was the first nuke and Washington was the first boomer. They deserve to be recognized and remembered."

"Indeed they do." That observation came from a tall gent who took a seat next to me. His hair was white, healthy but white, and the lines around his eyes were etched deep. High cheekbones on a thin face gave him a distinguished, almost diplomatic quality. He extended his hand. "Carl Wilson, though everyone here calls me Doc."

"Pleasure, Doc," I replied. "Jack Brouder."

Others appeared, men and women, and took their seats around the table. I nodded to them, in part to be polite and in part out of respect. Several wore hats or jackets bearing emblems representing past military service, service that preceded my stint in uniform. They fit the image: the honor guard at a Memorial Day parade, the squadron leaders at the VFW hall, the fortunate who served, survived and now meet to stay in touch and keep the memories alive.

The sound of laughter drew my attention. Several children bounced inside a play area set up at one end of the food court. Elsewhere mothers with children in tow were winding through a gauntlet of tables and chairs, pushing strollers past fast-food eateries of every description and heading off in various directions.

"Kind of early for the kids to show up," I noted.

"Snow day," Tom replied. "Too nasty outside to hold class but that doesn't keep mom from doing some shopping and bringing the toddlers along. Let's them burn off some energy."

I half-smiled. "I'm guilty of that myself, I suppose. Normally I'd be walking outside but it's too much hassle when the sidewalks get slick and the roads fill with slush. Walking here is my fallback plan. Been doing it a lot lately."

"Always good to have a Plan B," Doc said, "though I imagine the same view day after day would become a little monotonous."

He was right, yet as a veteran mall walker, I felt the need to defend my pastime. "It's not too bad. I let my mind wander, looking back over the years while my feet do all the work. And just like being outdoors the scenery here changes with the season."

I pointed up, where over-sized ornaments still dangled from colorful yard-wide ribbons. "Christmas is good for a couple months, then the Easter Bunny shows up for photos. Stores come and go and window displays get reworked for each new fashion trend. In the wintertime, the lower level becomes a new car showroom and in summer they bring in power boats and turn it into a make-shift marina. A constant state of change, if you will. It provides some variety, enough for me at least. I do two loops of each level but reverse direction for the second loop; things look different the second time around."

I searched for something to add, anything to make my justification seem less pathetic. "And it gives me a chance to ponder the great mysteries of mall life. Why do only some mannequins have heads? Why are they dressed in bathing suits while it's still snowing outside? And my personal favorite ... would anyone actually wear that outfit in public? These are things great philosophers have debated over the ages and I feel it is my duty to take up the quest."

At least Doc smiled. "Very noble of you," he replied.

"How long were you in for?" Tom asked.

"Twenty years. Joined up fresh out of college, back in '62. Korea was winding down, Vietnam was heating up, the draft loomed and I figured that if I had to serve it might as well be on my terms. Went to OCS, spent two years in the Supply Corps for the surface fleet but then volunteered for sub duty and they assigned me to the Washington as a Supply Officer. Made several patrols in the Atlantic before they shifted us to the Pacific. Eventually, the older boats were taken out of service as part of the SALT Treaty and I was reassigned to shore duty. That was fine with me; having my feet on solid ground gave me a chance to finish my MBA. I retired as a commander about the time I outlived my usefulness there. No regrets though, I was ready for a change. The experience was invaluable and the money I saved let me start my own business. I did okay, being my own boss but twenty-plus years of that was enough. I sold the business last year and now focus on staying young."

# Jeff Russell

That was it, my life history in sixty seconds, every plan carried out to completion. It was success as I imagined it and yet now my days are spent walking in circles because I have nothing better to do.

Doc smiled politely but looked at me as if there was more to the story. He had analytic eyes, compassionate but analytic, the type of eyes that look beyond the exterior, probing a person's conscience to search out whatever might be troubling them.

"We see you pass by now and then," he said. "You always nod … and you're always alone. Family nearby?"

The best I could manage was a sigh. "None. My military years were spent climbing in rank, always focused on the next promotion, always taking the tough assignments, whatever would move me ahead. And I saw what happened to families when mom was stuck home with the kids while dad was away on patrol. It was really tough for them, especially when dad was reassigned and the family had to relocate. New homes, new schools, old friends lost. Pulled up from your roots with little chance to make new ones. It was tough, I'm sure, and I didn't see the point in adding to that misery."

I paused to sip my coffee and reflect on what, in retrospect, may have been the first in a string of mistakes. "Always figured I'd settle down after getting out but then I started the business – ARQ Solutions, I developed custom logistic solutions – and it took over my life. Don't get me wrong, I loved the role, the responsibility, everything about the job … but I traveled constantly, leaving on short notice for extended stays of unpredictable duration. An itinerary like that makes it difficult to develop meaningful relationships. Came close once but … well, that didn't work out."

It was there again, a twinge of regret, of culpability, the inescapable reminder that some mistakes cannot be forgiven. I shook it off.

"On the bright side, having no strings attached makes it easy to do things on my schedule and within my budget. I've watched friends struggle to balance love and life, and I've seen the stress that accompanies their happiness. For better or worse my professional credo of 'never settle' somehow evolved into 'never settle down.' I don't know … maybe I should have done things differently … but it's too late now. Now, if I get lonely, I go for a walk and sometimes end up here. I'm not a big fan of crowds but being here, being around other people helps … especially during the holidays."

It occurred to me that I'd been talking, uninhibited and unrestrained, for too long. By now there were a dozen or so of them sitting at the table, all staring at me. My gaze shifted from one onlooker to the next as I tried reading their thoughts. Was I the interloper who barged in on their club meeting? The braggart who loved drawing attention to himself? I had shared information previously reserved for close friends and could only assume that my conduct today was the byproduct of their past military experience and my current lack of close friends.

"Let me introduce you to the rest of the table," Doc said.

I checked my watch. "Um … actually, I'd better get going. I have an appointment with my real-estate agent."

"Buying or selling?" Tom asked.

"Selling. I'm shipping out soon, couple of weeks perhaps."

"Brighter horizons, I hope," Doc said.

I tried to smile. "We'll see."

Once again I felt him looking beyond the exterior. "Well, until then feel free to join us any time. We're here most mornings and would love to chat again."

Something about his invitation struck a chord as if he – perhaps all of them – had at one time or another faced an uncertain future and found clarity in companionship. I was there now, poised on the precipice of an uncertain future with part of me arguing that I hadn't given it enough thought, that I should be seeking the counsel of those who had been there before rather than going it alone. I had always gone it alone, at least as far as my personal life was concerned, and yet some of my decisions – especially those made in the absence of wiser counsel, where my opinion was the only one I sought – had not worked out for the best.

She called me a recluse … and I didn't want her to be right on that count. "I'd like that," I replied.

## Chapter 2

Doc spotted me first. I had drifted toward their table, coffee in hand, when he waved me over. Tom shifted to the left and pulled another chair up to make room. I took the seat.

"We were just talking about you the other day," Doc said. "We've got folks here from all branches of the service, including the Navy, but none have ever been on a boomer. What's it like to be stuck underwater for a couple months at a time?"

There were ten others present, all currently focused on me. Some leaned in my direction and it occurred to me that answering the question meant speaking loud enough for everyone to hear. I took a sip of coffee and peered over the rim of the cup. The audience appeared interested, always a good sign and so I launched into a speech I'd put together earlier in the day just in case.

"Morning everyone. For the record, I'm Jack Brouder, USN retired and former business owner who now spends his leisure time trying to keep the heart pumping and the pounds off. The last time I was here I blabbed on for a while so if that happens again just throw something in my direction. I'll get the hint. Um ... to answer Doc's question, being on patrol wasn't all that bad. The Washington was an FBM – a Fleet Ballistic Missile boat – and our job was to stay out at sea, cruise around in circles and be quiet, usually for sixty days at a time. Back then, it may have changed by now, but back then the FBMs had two crews – Blue and Gold. We took turns on the boat, spending one month getting ready to go out to sea and two months on patrol before swapping off with the other crew. During our off-time we were on shore with our families, usually attending training of some form. The two months spent at sea didn't seem that long, at least to me. There was plenty of work to keep everyone busy, the occasional drill and a different movie to watch every night. The movies were on sixteen-millimeter film – all we had at the time – and we showed them in the mess decks after mid-rats. We didn't have the luxury of port calls or re-supplies so milk was powdered and perishables were frozen but despite that, we actually ate quite well." I smiled, hoping to lighten the mood. "Of course as the Supply Officer, I made sure we always got the good stuff."

"How did you stay in touch with your family when you were underwater?" someone asked.

I nodded to acknowledge the question, grateful to have others join in the discussion. "Not many options there. Once we left for patrol we were under radio silence, which meant we could not send messages. We could receive them but they came in on a low-frequency signal, very slow, so any 'family-grams' – as we called them – had to be kept short. The guys understood, it was part of the job. And they knew that the captain and XO's wives would keep in touch with the rest of the wives, and many of the wives would hang-out together on a regular basis. They were a family of their own while the boat was away. If anything went wrong at home we knew that someone was there to help."

Doc went next. "It must have been pretty tight quarters. Ever have any fights on board?"

"None that I've ever experienced. The majority of the crew were enlisted, they all ate in the same mess and bunked in the same compartment. Everyone knew everyone else, knew that each man had a unique job and that all jobs were necessary to keep the boat running so they pretty much got along. Playful rivalries were the norm but so was professional respect."

"Any scary times?" another asked.

"Nothing exciting, if that's what you mean. A small fire once – electrical if I remember correctly – but that's not a big deal. You cut the power, hit it with some CO2 and vent the area through the air scrubbers. I remember one time when we had an actual flooding incident. We had come up to periscope depth to listen for incoming radio messages. Whenever we did that we'd run the diesel engine to keep it tuned-up. All nuke boats have a diesel as a backup power source and for emergency ventilation. If we had a major fire and the boat filled with smoke, or hydrogen gas escaped from the battery well or there was a radiation release in the reactor compartment we could come to periscope depth, raise the snorkel and run the diesel. It sucked air from inside the boat, which created a vacuum that pulled outside air down the snorkel mast and into the fan room. From there the fresh air would be channeled into all compartments. It's usually very effective but on this one occasion, things didn't go to plan. The snorkel head has a large 'flapper' valve that shuts if a wave washes over it, thus preventing water from being sucked into the fan room. Our valve failed and the room flooded. Fortunately, it was designed for that possibility and no damage was done but the flooding alarm sounded anyway – any uncontrolled intake of water is considered a flood – and everyone jumped to their assigned duty stations. As I said, nothing too exciting. We trained for things like that and no one panicked if something went wrong."

A head leaned forward from the far end of the table. "What do you think about the proposal to let women serve on submarines?"

This time I grinned. "That's an easy one … I *don't* think about it. I can't begin to imagine the logistics involved, or worse yet having guys explain that situation to their wives."

Something amazing happened then. They laughed. Everyone laughed.

"I think introductions are in order," Doc said. "You've already met Tom, so starting to my left we'll go counter-clockwise around the table. This is Harris, Gus, Dent, John, Vic, Will, Mac and his wife Millie, and finally Don and his wife Jan. Gus, Dent, Harris and I are Army. Mac is Marine. Don, Will, and Tom are Navy and Vic is Air Force. I hope you're taking notes because there will be a test at the end of the meeting."

I was busy associating names with faces and service branches when Doc's last comment registered. When I glanced at him he winked.

"Do you meet every day?" I asked.

"Pretty much, but informally. We come when it's convenient, when we have no other obligations and would like to sit and chat for a while. You can always count on one of us being here. I don't think I've ever arrived and found that I was the only one in attendance."

I looked around the table and nodded. "So you're a group that meets informally just to stay in touch, like a family. That's nice, actually. Is it 'The Guys' ... or does your group have a name?"

No one spoke. I scanned their faces, waiting for an answer. Everyone was staring back at me. Doc tried to adopt a serious expression but I caught him hiding a smile. "You've heard of the Order of Elks, the Ancient Order of Hibernians, the Order of Omega?"

"Um ... yes."

"Well," he said, "We are the Perpetual Order of Old People."

I took a moment to digest that. "Okay, sounds pretty formal for an informal group."

The others were still looking at me as if anticipating my reaction, and I had to think back to what I had missed.

"What?" I asked, frowning. Then it hit me.

"Wait ... Perpetual Order of Old People."

I hesitated before saying it.

"P-O-O-P ... Poop?"

All eyes shifted to Gus, who looked as if I'd violated some sacred law. He yanked off his cap, a tattered remnant embroidered with two crossed cannons – the US Army Artillery insignia – and threw it down on the table. Massive eyebrows and thick tufts of white hair above his ears framed an otherwise bald head that reflected the overhead lights. He gritted his teeth, pointed a clenched fist in my direction and then pounded it down hard on the table. I felt the vibration in my stomach.

"We ain't poop!" he almost yelled. "We're just old farts!"

Then he threw his head back and laughed, a long, loud belly-laugh that left him out of breath as if he'd just told the funniest joke in the world. Doc looked down and rocked his head from side to side, embarrassed perhaps by the outburst, while the others just smiled. Apparently, they'd heard that joke before.

"You compared us to a family," Doc said, turning to me. "In many ways that's true. A family might meet around the dinner table, mom and dad relating their hectic days, sons and daughters talking about school and sports, individuals coming together to share their lives because it feels good to know that someone cares. Then after that, they return to their separate agendas. We do the same thing here."

# The Perpetual Order of Old People

"Yeah," Harris added. "Only difference is we meet to gripe about arthritis and Medicare." That observation prompted a unanimous chuckle.

"And grandkids," Dent said, holding up his cell phone. "Don't forget the grandkids!" He turned the display toward the rest of us and I glimpsed the image of several youngsters gathered around him. I also noted the look on Dent's face. There was pride in his smile and confidence in his eyes, the type of confidence that said old age isn't relevant because life goes on. I envied him.

"Great thing about grandkids," Harris noted, "is that you get to spoil them and then send them home to let mom and dad deal with the ramifications. Payback time!"

"Got that right!"

I looked across to see who said that and half the guys were grinning. Could have been any of them … or all of them.

"Any grandkids?" I asked Doc.

"Four. Three local and one in Vermont. We see him often though – just a few hours from here. Nice day trip."

"We?"

"My wife, Kate. She comes to these meetings now and then but most days she oversees a volunteer group at the hospital. Says it keeps her young and she knows I'll stay out of trouble if I come here. I volunteer there on the afternoon shift and then at night we compare notes."

Doc, I was certain, had at least ten years on me. He spoke with the confidence and clarity of an educated man but his voice was subdued, guarded as if there was no longer any power behind it. Yet despite those outward signs I now felt old in comparison. There was purpose in his life and he kept himself young because he still had a job to do. My contribution to mankind was a thing of the past.

"Okay gents," Gus said while standing. "Time for me to shove off. See you tomorrow."

"See ya," someone said.

"Give Emma our best," another added.

Gus nodded in return, then headed off toward the parking garage. He walked with a pronounced limp as if one leg struggled to keep up. I was transfixed by the sight, wondering if that's what happens as the body ages, as individual components fail and fall behind. And I wondered if a person grows accustomed to it, whether simple maladies become so routine that they are no longer noticed … or whether they pile up, one on the next until every effort becomes a struggle. They say that life beats the alternative and I wondered if I would still agree when it came my time to bear the burden of old age.

Tom leaned closer as Gus drifted away. "War injury, though he won't talk about it."

"And Emma?" I asked.

"His wife. She's in Brookside Health Care, been there for about eight years now. Paralyzed from the waist down; took a bad fall I think … really sad. Gus spends every day with her after leaving here. They watch TV, talk about old times and flip through photo albums reliving the past. He calls her the love of his life and I believe him."

"We all do," Doc added. "Don't let his snarly demeanor fool you. When it comes to his wife he's a softy."

He checked his watch and then downed the rest of his coffee. "I should be going too," he announced to the table. "Promised to pick up groceries before reporting for duty today."

I stood with him and we shook hands. "Glad you were able to join us this morning," he said. "We'd like to hear more about your adventures under the sea. Drop in anytime, we're here just about every day."

As if taking their cue from Doc's departure the others drifted off in turn. A backslap, a playful shoulder-punch, Harris, and Dent even mimicked a missed high-five as friends bid each other farewell for the day. In the end, only Tom and I remained.

A quiet settled over the table, the quiet that precedes a difficult discussion.

"Wife paralyzed, huh?" I said, shaking my head. "That's gotta be tough. At least they have each other."

Tom nodded. "Yeah, you never know what life's gonna throw at you. Be grateful for family, I keep telling myself."

He stared away for a while, perhaps thinking about his. Then he turned to me. "Got any?"

I was looking out the window, past the corner of the parking garage and into a cold winter sky. A lifetime of self-centered progressions left me financially secure but alone and any day now life could throw a hardball in my direction. I had dwelled on that scenario for the better part of the past year, trying to decide whether to duck or risk catching it. By the time Tom's question sank in I'd forgotten what we were talking about.

"Sorry, what?"

"Got any family?"

Some simple questions have difficult answers. I forced a smile. "Molly and Connor, my sister's kids. They live out west, close to where they grew up." Whatever I went to say next caught in my throat.

"Do you see them often?" Tom asked.

I shrugged. "That depends on how you define often. Is twice in three years not enough when I'm the only senior citizen left in the family?" I bowed my head in penance. "Molly's a real sweetheart but she tends to micro-manage the people around her. It's not that she wants to be the boss, I think rather she is just so full of energy and confident in her abilities and eager to help that she takes over automatically. The bigger the affair the more excited she becomes and soon she's assigning roles and handing out agendas. That's great if she's working *for* you … but I like choosing my own chores and schedule. Know what I mean?"

# The Perpetual Order of Old People

Tom replied with an understanding nod.

"Went out there for Connor's wedding and several times after that to visit. Molly had me booked from the moment I arrived. Thought of putting my foot down but I could see how important being the activities director was to her and I didn't have the heart. Couldn't wait to get back home though."

"Well," Tom said, "if visits are a rare occasion then perhaps you can indulge her passion for the sake of being with family."

The chance to meet others, share my story and listen to theirs left me unusually upbeat this morning but now I felt that energy being siphoned away by the ghost of things to come.

"Yeah, well that's the problem. They want me to move out there, to Phoenix, and be with them permanently. Molly works for a non-profit that's having some issues and she's convinced their board that I can help ... so now *they* want me to come out. She assures me this job won't drain the hours from my day like my old job."

I took a sip of coffee. "Connor is a great guy, good head on his shoulders. He was really close to his mom and wants to stay close to her side of the family. I'm the only one left. His wife though ... she's a piece of work. Tessa wants me out there to make sure I don't do something foolish like run off with a lady friend and leave my inheritance to someone else."

# Jeff Russell

It was a subject I tried not to think about and began to regret bringing it up. Soon it was there again, the churning in my stomach and the taste of acid on my breath.

"I like Connor, and I have high expectations for him, but I don't think I can tolerate being around his wife for any length of time. '*We need a new car. Connor needs a better job. We'll never save enough to put the kids through college.*' Two minutes of that and I'm ready to go for a walk and not come back."

I'd done it again, let the private side of me out, and began to regret that also. There are chinks in everyone's armor and I prefer not to expose mine but I think Tom had already caught a glimpse.

"So don't move," he said. "You seem to be doing alright on your own."

It was a chess move and well played. I could see the anticipation in his eyes, in his raised eyebrows. He was waiting for my response. I surrendered my piece.

"Doing okay now, maybe, but not getting any younger. Sooner or later age catches up with all of us. I've seen what happens to some people. They end up in nursing homes, bedridden and helpless, cared for by strangers. No family, no visitors, no future … only the same hell day after day. I tell myself it won't happen to me, that I love my independence too much and won't let that happen but who am I kidding? I'm sure that every resident of every nursing home has said the same thing at one point."

# The Perpetual Order of Old People

"Famous last words," Tom said. "Tragedies begin with the words '*That'll never happen to me.*'"

My coffee had gone cold. I considered getting another but didn't want to stop talking. I'd exposed my deepest chink and talking about it felt like the right thing to do. I trusted Tom; my secret was safe with him.

"Maybe I'll be lucky. Maybe I'll go while I'm still in my prime and won't have to worry about those feeble years. Or maybe I'll stay sharp and agile long after I've stopped serving a purpose and pass away peacefully in my sleep. But if I *do* end up in a nursing home I don't want it to be here, alone. At least out west Molly and Connor would visit me, and he'd bring the kids. They're super kids and I'd make sure they're taken care of. At least then I'll still feel useful. And if I do it while I'm still young I can be the grandpa they've never had. I'd like to be a grandpa."

I leaned back in my chair. "So there's the dilemma: stay here and risk dying a bored, lonely miser, or move out west where Molly can make my to-do list and Tessa can suck the blood from my bank account." I laughed at myself for saying that; it would have been corny if it hadn't been true.

"Listen to me, talking like an old …" I caught myself before saying it aloud but I'm sure Tom read my mind. "An old fool," I continued. "I'm going to Phoenix. A phoenix is supposed to rise from the ashes, right? My life may be heading for a crash and burn here but moving provides an opportunity to rise from the ashes and start over. Maybe I'll get it right this time."

We sat in silence while an uncertain future played out in my mind.

"Is it selfish of me to want family and independence at the same time?"

Tom shook his head. "No … it's human. But you still have to choose. Any idea what you're going to do?"

I drew in a long breath and let it out slowly. "I heard from my agent yesterday. They want to set a closing date."

"You don't look very happy about it," he remarked.

The walk home was haunted by visions of my grandfather imprisoned behind the concrete walls of an inner-city nursing home, confined to a rusted steel-railed bed in a room with a dozen other rusted beds, each occupied by the shadow of a once vibrant life. Some moaned, others spoke incomprehensibly, most lay silently with their eyes closed or staring blankly at the ceiling. In the next room, other lost souls were being spoon fed something ladled into bowls from a large cauldron. Those who could swallow did so with contempt, and only after much bickering, while those who couldn't let it drool out of their open mouth and down their chin. Such was my introduction to the final resting place of a life that wasn't done living.

*That'll never happen to me*, I heard myself say.

# The Perpetual Order of Old People

## Chapter 3

Neat rows of salmon filets waited on a field of crushed ice in the display case. I closed my eyes and pictured one, sautéed and with a creamy dill sauce sitting on my dinner plate alongside garlic mashed potatoes and grilled asparagus. Fish had been missing from my meal plan lately, a clear violation of my edict to maintain a healthy diet, so I added it to this week's menu. A tapping sound on the glass partition beyond the deli counter brought me back to the present and I looked up. Butch waved from the back room, wiped his hands on his apron and mouthed the words '*Be right out.*' A short while later we stood face-to-face.

"Afternoon Jack, What'll it be today?"

"Hi, Butch. Think I'll give the chateaubriand another try. I trust you've got some nice tenderloin back there?"

"Only the best for my best customers. Something go wrong the last time?"

Some people pour their heart out to the bartender but I have someone actually qualified to give advice. My frown was part plea, part embarrassed smirk. "The meat came out great - thanks for the searing tip by the way – but my sauce still needs work. The reduction was a little thin and I probably went overboard with the shallots. And the taste still isn't right, it's too … tart."

"What wine did you use?"

"Sauvignon blanc."

He nodded. "Crisp, but perhaps a little too acidic. Try a pinot gris and let the sauce simmer longer, slowly. Give it time to reduce and let the flavors blend. And go easy on the shallots."

I stored the revised recipe in my head, hoping it would still be there later. "Thanks. I'll keep trying until I get it right."

One raised eyebrow. "And how will you know when you've got it right?"

It might simply have been a warm atmosphere on a cold Chicago night, or the attractive waitress who took the time to converse with a lonely businessman, or even the glass of cabernet I enjoyed before the entrée arrived, but I credit the magic of that evening to the mouth-watering chateaubriand at a little French restaurant on West Adams. It set the standard for all others.

"I'll know," I said, smiling.

Butch smiled then as well. "Sounds good. How big a slice would you like?"

A simple shrug. "You know me … table for one."

The sauce was simmering, slowly, as Butch advised, when the phone rang. I frowned, grabbing the phone with one hand while continuing to stir with the other. Anxiety slipped into my voice as I spoke.

"Hello?"

"Hi, Uncle Jack. It's Molly!"

My eyes crimped closed and I had to force them open again to maintain watch over the sauce.

# The Perpetual Order of Old People

"Hi, Mol … hold on a sec, I need to turn this down."

"Am I interrupting?"

"No, no … just preparing dinner."

"Yum, smells good from here. What's on the menu?"

"Chateaubriand. I'm playing with the sauce recipe, trying to get it perfect."

"It doesn't come in a bottle?" There was a hint of playful kidding in her question.

"Where's the fun in that?" I asked. "So, what's up?"

"I was wondering if you had time for a quick question. Well … maybe not that quick."

The urge to ask if we might reschedule succumbed to better judgment. *Be grateful for family,* someone whispered in my ear. I turned off the skillet and hoped for the best.

"Of course. What's on your mind?"

She waited before responding. "You knew Mom before she married Dad. How did she know he was the one?"

My hand trembled as I reached for a chair. I needed to sit, to let the flood of memories wash in and recede, as they always do when the subject came up. Peter's death in a car accident on his way home from work devastated their small family but Karen stepped up and took over, the single parent raising two young children and teaching them that life must go on. No doubt that lesson made it easier for Molly and Conner twelve years later when their mom succumbed to cancer. I shook it off and tried to focus on the question.

"Your mom was a lot like you growing up. She was smart, energetic and determined. And she never settled … not in school, not in sports, not in anything she did. I've never met anyone with more self-confidence. She knew what she wanted, knew a good deal when she saw it and she went for it. She was also very popular with the boys, no problem getting invites to a dance or movie, but she was picky about who she dated. 'Only the good guys,' she once told me. I met most of them, wanted to be the protective big brother, and she was right … they were good guys, though she didn't take them too seriously. I think she knew something better was out there. I first met your dad when I was home on leave and it was clear from the start that she treated him differently. She watched and waited, taking her time to see if he recognized that she was special too. He did. To answer your question, I believe she knew he was the one when they started talking to each other with their eyes, and their smiles, and the way they held hands."

Images of Karen and Peter wrapped in each other's arms filled my head. I let them sway for a while. "This may sound strange coming from a life-long bachelor but watching your mom and dad together while they were dating was probably the first time I recognized that kind of affection, that kind of love."

During the long pause that followed, I wondered if anything I told her made sense.

# The Perpetual Order of Old People

"Have you ever felt that way about anyone?" she asked.

The memory was there. I tried thinking my way around it, looking for alternatives but kept coming back to the same place.

"Yeah, maybe … once. But that's ancient history … like me."

"Ha! You're not ancient, Uncle Jack. There's still time to shop around. What would you look for in that someone special?"

It was a good question, one for which a good answer was not readily available. I tried anyway. "Well, for starters she'd have to turn a blind eye to my many faults." Another thought came to mind and I adopted a more serious approach. "And there would have to be trust, both ways. I can tell you from experience that trust is critical in business situations and I imagine it must be infinitely more so in romance. There must be complete and unequivocal trust."

I glanced to the side, where the skillet was still waiting for me. "And there must be patience. Every individual brings their own unique flavors to a relationship and it takes time for those flavors to blend. Both parties must want perfection and be willing to take the time, tweaking the recipe until they get it right."

That last observation sounded uncharacteristically philosophical, even for me, and I wondered if old age had started smoothing out my rough edges.

"Why all these questions?" I asked.

"Oh, just wondering. I'll let you get back to your cooking. Save some for me!"

I looked back at the skillet. *Just wondering?*

The sauce did come out better; not perfect but a creation I would happily serve to guests. And until such time that I actually had guests over for dinner, I would continue to tweak the recipe. The latest version, revised minutes earlier, included pulling it from the stove to let it thicken a bit while waiting for the flavors to blend.

After cleaning the kitchen I faced the dilemma of how to spend the remainder of the evening. Packing was the obvious choice. A stack of folded shipping cartons leaned against a wall, waiting to be assembled and filled. Meanwhile, half a lifetime of possessions, some of which had not been touched since the move here from my previous residence, waited to be sorted. Some would go west, some would be donated and the rest would be trashed. It was a simple process that for some reason I've always dreaded. A great deal of thought and effort went into buying and caring for each individual item – everything from clothing, books and kitchen gadgets to the elaborate stereo system that I hooked up but seldom use – and the thought of leaving anything behind is inextricably linked to the fear that someday I'll regret not having it. Making such decisions calls for the proper frame of mind and I knew I wasn't there tonight. Between the challenges of chateaubriand and Molly's

# The Perpetual Order of Old People

curious conversation, this day had already seen its share of complications. Tonight would be better spent in some form of relaxation.

A best-seller that hadn't yet impressed me waited by the armchair while a partially completed thousand-piece jigsaw puzzle covered one end of the coffee table and a chess board sat at the other end. I moved to the chess board and examined the pieces, trying to recall which color I played the last time and what strategy I had in mind. When I couldn't remember I flipped a coin. Heads is white – I would play white tonight. I tried but my mind wasn't in the game, it was back on the phone call with Molly, wondering what prompted her question and what mischief she was up to this time.

## Chapter 4

It may have been the recent stretch of wintry weather or the minor aches and pains that appear lately when I consider taking an aggressive walk but for whatever reason I found myself drawn back to the mall, arriving early and showing up at the group table. I felt relaxed, like I belonged there, like I was welcome. The situation was temporary – I was transient, one foot out the door – but as with so many jobs for so many clients over the years I relished the opportunity to interact with others.

Some members were already present and in their assigned seats. It was a trait I'd seen in the past and accepted as human nature – people who come together on a recurring basis tend to arrange themselves in a set order around the table. I opted to rock the boat by taking a different seat today than the one I occupied yesterday. Staying random, spontaneous and unpredictable would make my absence less noticeable when the time came.

The older gent to my left turned to me and extended his hand. "Hi, I'm Will. You were Navy, right?"

He was tall, even when seated, and bore the greying hair and furrowed brow that marked people of his generation, yet he had youthful eyes that brimmed with enthusiasm. I shook his hand eagerly.

"Hi Will … Jack. Yes, Navy for twenty years, though it seems like a lifetime ago."

"Same here," he replied. "Though my hitch was only for a couple years and feels like two lifetimes ago."

# The Perpetual Order of Old People

"During the war?" I asked.

He nodded.

I shifted my seat to face him. "What was that like?"

His eyes appeared to get younger as if revisiting old memories turned back the years. "I was drafted in February of '44, just 18 years old at the time. They put me on a bus headed for New Haven, where a Marine sergeant asked me what branch of the service I wanted. I told him the Navy and he instructed me to go stand in a long line. After a while, he called me back and asked again what branch I wanted and again I told him the Navy. Once more he told me to go stand in that line. Then he called me back a third time and said 'I think you would make a great Marine. We need Marines.' Well, I had a brother in the Marines and he said it was tough. I had another brother in the Navy and he liked it there so I said 'Look, I want the Navy.' Finally, he sent me back to the Navy line and left me there. Glad I stuck to my guns."

"I can imagine," I replied. "The Navy did right by me. Recruiting stations can be a bit intimidating, especially when the draft is looming over your head, but if you want to have any say in your future then you have to speak up. Where did you do your basic training?"

"Sampson, New York. They had a Naval Training Station there at the time but I think the Air Force took it over after the war. We were there for five weeks – a lot of training in a short time – and after that I got two weeks leave. I was told I scored well on some tests and would be sent to specialized training, but next thing I know I'm standing on Pier 92 in New York getting ready to board the Queen Mary. She took us to Southampton, England. From there I was assigned to LST-2 as a Radioman striker, even though I hadn't received any training on the equipment. I learned everything on the job."

"What's an LST?" I asked.

"Landing Ship/Tank. It was a big, flat-bottom boat with bow doors that swung open to let tanks and other large vehicles drive in and out. We made thirty trips across the English Channel from Southampton to the beaches of Normandy during Phase 2 of the invasion. They called the LST a 'slow-moving barge' because that's what it was … slow. Top speed was only about ten knots so each trip took a couple of days. At least things were a little better going from England to Normandy. On the out-bound trip we carried fresh troops – soldiers and Marines – but we were also loaded down with tanks and other heavy vehicles. Those were stored on the lower level – what we called the 'tank deck' – and that helped keep the ship steady in the water. On the return trip, we only carried wounded GIs and German POWs. Without the weight of the heavy vehicles, the ship sat on top of the water and got pummeled by the waves. The seas in the Channel were rough most of the time and an LST, being flat-bottomed, was not very stable in the water. We were always worried about getting swamped. I'll tell you something, you wouldn't last five minutes in that water … too cold."

"Don't think I'd want to know what that's like," I admitted.

He shook his head solemnly and I wonder if he had friends, shipmates from the past who learned the hard way. Despite an aversion for such thoughts, I saw myself caught in that scenario, the instantaneous shock of numbing cold, arms and legs thrashing even as muscles begin to cramp, overwhelmed by the weight of water-soaked clothing, lungs screaming for air and head straining to reach a surface that is slowly drifting away. Then silence … followed by the haunting acceptance that whatever turmoil existed on the surface, whatever lives were being shattered and blood was being spilled no longer mattered. For this soul, the war was over.

"Thirty cycles of that sounds a bit unnerving."

Will started to smile but it faded quickly, never quite reaching his eyes. "That was the easy part. A good captain can deal with the waves. The real threat at sea came from German E-boats."

I did a quick search of my memory banks and came up empty. "Not familiar with those," I told him.

He nodded with the confidence of someone all too familiar with them. "An E-boat was a German torpedo boat, like the American PT-boats but larger. They were fast with a long operating range. We would always leave in a convoy of twenty to thirty ships and lose two or three on each crossing to E-boats. You knew they were out there, knew someone was going to get hit and all you could do was hope it wouldn't be you."

He thought a moment longer. "And being in Normandy wasn't any picnic. The whole point of having an LST is to get the vehicles directly from the ship to the shore. To do that we had to wait for high tide, go in as close as we could get and then drop anchor and wait for the tide to go out again. Eventually, the ship would bottom in the sand. We'd swing open the bow doors to let the tanks and trucks drive up onto the beach. Once that was done and the infantry had gone ashore we would load the troops and prisoners going back to England and then wait for high tide so we could get underway again. All this time we were sitting ducks for the German 150-millimeter gun emplacements that sat in the hills overlooking the beach. The Navy tried knocking them out before the invasion but those guns were heavily fortified and some remained operational. They started shooting as soon as we got there. Several of my friends were injured that way. This one time I left the radio shack and went down to the tank deck to get a cup of coffee and while I was gone the shack took a direct hit. I never heard a noise that loud before. Blew away everything. If I hadn't gone for that coffee I wouldn't be sitting here today."

"Timing is everything," I said. "So tell me … you made thirty trips out and back across the Channel, hunted by E-boats, at the mercy of the seas and grounded within range of the German guns. Did it ever get routine? Did you ever get accustomed to the idea that this time it might be your turn to not make it back?"

He shook his head, then looked away. "Never. You never stopped worrying about that."

From the corner of my eye, I saw others looking our way, listening to Will, perhaps waiting to hear what other memories he might volunteer. They knew, I'm sure, the therapeutic value of reliving the triumphs and confronting the demons of the past.

Eventually, he turned back to me. "After the war, they decommissioned the ship and gave it to England. Sure hope they took good care of her. But they didn't decommission me. I was sent to Fort Pierce in Florida for amphibious training – something I never actually used – and then they promoted me to Electricians Mate Third Class and made me Chief Operator of a Clover telephone exchange on Okinawa. They left me there until May of '46 and then discharged me."

It was like watching a movie of a young man being forced to age a lifetime in the span of a few short years – the drama, the apprehension, the fear, rough seas, torpedoes, shells exploding – all pulled from six decades of memories.

"You have amazing recall," I told him.

Then he smiled again. "Some details … the ones that define your life … they stick with you."

It occurred to me that the table was quiet, and as I looked around I saw that everyone was watching and listening to Will, caught up in a tale they had probably heard before. That didn't matter. Memories – even familiar ones – can rekindle a flame that burns bright even after the body has burned out. Will shared his story, and while I could tell by the look in his eyes that he was proud of his past it was also obvious that the others present enjoyed going along for the ride, sharing a gift that goes both ways.

That was enough for one day. I bid my friends an early adieu and went for a walk to reflect on what Will said. His was just one story and while other group members might have their own tale to tell I did not want to risk hearing them all at once and confusing the facts. Will's chronicle of one man's war was unique and deserved to be remembered that way.

Soon I began comparing his story to mine, searching for those exhilarating details that defined my life. It was a short list. I received a commission as an officer but in retrospect overseeing supplies seemed trivial when compared to transporting men and machinery to the war front. I served onboard a submarine but today's submarines are among the safest vessels ever built and no one was shooting at us. I gave twenty years of my life in service to my country but the government paid me back twenty times over in advancements and opportunities. That could not equate to those who gave their life for their country. For all the time I served I never once felt at risk. Will, on the other hand, faced it constantly. Sixty crossings, each with two possible

# The Perpetual Order of Old People

outcomes – either survive to do it again or perish. Where does one find the courage? Was it youth? Do you not seriously consider the possibility of death while waiting to start living your life? Was it war? Does the prospect of losing, of ceasing to exist as a free country and falling subject to a foreign power give you the strength to push fear out of your mind?  Was it the pride of knowing that your contribution, no matter how large or small, would help write a critical chapter in the history of the world? These were all good questions … questions I should be asking.

It occurred to me that night, while sorting, packing and tossing, that I looked forward to the next day. It may simply have been the reward of distraction, thinking about the future to free myself from the drudgery of chores at hand. Or it may have been the stories, those first-hand accounts of danger, daring and drama that transport me to a world far more exciting than my own and add spice to a life that has become bland and tasteless. But if I had to pin a cause on my anticipation I would choose hope, for I had come to regret some decisions made in the absence of wiser counsel and right now, with a monumental decision pending, the collective genius of a few old men who meet each day for coffee was the closest thing I had to wisdom.

Whatever the reason, tomorrow could not arrive soon enough.

# Chapter 5

The following morning I took a seat across from Mac, one of the older gents in the group. His face was drawn as if the years had siphoned some of the life away, but his dancing blue-grey eyes invited conversation. A Marine Corps hat suggested pride in his service background and an ever-present smile told me he might have a tale to tell. I extended my hand. "Hi. I'm Jack," I started.

His handshake surprised me. It was soft bordering on weak but warm at the same time. "Nice to meet you, Jack. I'm Harry Gilmore." He maintained eye contact, perhaps waiting on my reaction.

"Harry?" I asked, suddenly concerned that I'd gotten his name wrong.

Tom, who was sitting to my left, leaned closer. "Don't let him kid you. It's Mac, but he goes by Harry when he submits cornball articles to the paper. Darned if I understand why but sometimes they actually get printed." Then he nodded across the way. "Morning Mac," he said. "How you doing today?"

Mac, or Harry … whoever he was … made a sour face. "Not so good. I've got an enlarged alimony."

"He means he *should* have an enlarged alimony," Gus remarked. "Millie's a saint for putting up with him." Gus leaned forward to look beyond Mac to an attractive woman with a demure smile and neatly styled

# The Perpetual Order of Old People

silver hair sitting next to Mac. "Am I right, Millie?" he asked.

Her smile brightened and she looked at Mac, who then met her gaze. "Do I know you?" she asked.

"I'm the love of your life," he responded.

Millie stared back momentarily. "Hmm … thought you looked familiar." Then she leaned forward and kissed him on the cheek.

Mac turned back to me and shrugged. "Selective amnesia," he said. "Sixty years of wedded bliss will do that to you."

"So, how long were you in the Marine Corps?" I asked.

He pulled his seat closer to the table and bent forward to speak over the background noise. "Just during the late war years. I signed up out of high school, as did most of my buddies. Went to Parris Island for training, then shipped out to Saipan, in the Pacific. After that, they moved our outfit to Tinian, which was a little south of Saipan. The Marines had just taken the island from the Japanese and the Seabees were building landing strips for the B-29s that would be used to bomb Japan. I was stationed there as part of an anti-aircraft crew to help defend the airfields. We manned a 90-millimeter gun." He formed a circle about three inches in diameter with his hands to show the size of the shell. "It was as big as they came for an AA battery back then."

Others were starting to listen in so I tried to keep the discussion moving. "Did you see any action?"

"Not from the enemy," he replied. "The Japs knew they weren't going to take those islands back and they didn't have the resources to send bombers that far just to try stopping us."

He smiled a bit at that point. "There was another, smaller island a few miles south of Tinian – the name was *Aguigan* I think … something like that. The Japs had a garrison stationed there but they didn't pose any threat so we left them alone. Every day they would raise their flag – the red sun on a white background – at a peak near the western side of the island. I figure they did that just to let us know they were still holding on. Now and then we'd train our gun on them to see if we could take down the flag. Our crew chief called it target practice. We always aimed for the flag … weren't trying to hurt anyone because there was really no point in that. I think we might have hit it once. It was pretty far away, about as far as our shells could travel horizontally. If we did hit it the Japs put up another pole and raised the flag again the next day. It became a game for us. Hope they felt the same way."

His eyes drifted to the side. "I have to give them credit, they held on even though they were cut off from the rest of the world. That garrison didn't surrender until after the war ended."

"So, was this a tropical paradise for you?" I inquired.

# The Perpetual Order of Old People

"The weather was certainly nice there," he replied. "Most of the time at least, so I guess in some ways it was a paradise. But even without incoming attacks, there was still plenty of work to do. I stood a lot of guard duty, and in fact, I was part of the detail that guarded the Enola Gay before she took off to bomb Hiroshima. We knew something special was going on because they took a lot of precautions loading her, had to do it differently from the other planes. None of us knew anything about the atomic bombs until later. It was a good thing, I guess … those two bombs … I truly believe they ended the war. Everyone expected an invasion of Japan, expected thousands more Americans to die fighting an enemy that refused to give up, but then the surrender came and it was time to go home."

He smiled at first but that faded quickly. "But it wasn't a paradise for everybody. A lot of Marines died taking Guam, Saipan, and Tinian from the Japanese. That was just a few months before I got there. An invasion like that is never a picnic. Their shore batteries would take out our landing craft, they had barbed wire strung up and down the beach and machine gun nests behind that. The Navy bombarded those islands before the shore landings but it wasn't enough. We had the Japs outnumbered but they hung on. They would rather die than surrender, and most of them did."

He paused to take a sip of coffee. "And it wasn't any fun for the Seabees, either. They had a pretty tough job building those airfields, plus the hangers and all the

45

associated facilities to house the troops. Did you know their name came from the letters C and B? Stood for Construction Battalion, which everyone just shortened to CB. At some point, not sure when, the letters got changed to the words *sea*, like in the ocean, and *bee*, like in bumblebee. Same thing happened with the jeep. It started out as the General Purpose vehicle, which then got shortened to the letters G and P, or GP, and everyone just started calling it the *jeep*. I suppose people do that because it's convenient, but I think they also like having a nickname. Makes it more personal. Anyway, the Seabees had to clear some pretty tough terrain, plus they didn't have a lot of time and when their equipment broke down there was a long wait for spare parts. But they got the job done."

His thin grey eyebrows creased as if weighed down by the sudden recall of a distant, melancholy memory. I waited, as did the others around the table.

"I imagine," he continued, "that it was hardest on the B-29 crews. Those planes always took off overloaded. They needed extra fuel to reach Japan and get back again, and they were always stuffed full of bombs. That was a bad combination, more payload than the plane was designed to carry. Some couldn't lift off when they reached the cliff at the end of the runway, they just disappeared over the edge and then crashed and burned all night. The crews knew this, knew that if all four engines didn't make maximum thrust that they were going down even before the mission started and there

# The Perpetual Order of Old People

would be no escape, no rescue. But every one of them wanted to fly, every pilot, navigator, bombardier, gunner and whoever else was onboard wanted to do their part. I got to know some of them personally and we always wished them luck, even kidded about it – you know, to take the tension off – but inside you wished they didn't have to go. Suppose that's the way it is in combat … you know you might die today but you're so focused on getting the job done that you manage to look past the fear."

He looked down at his hands, which were folded together on the table. They were large hands that had grown thin, robbed of their vitality, with dark veins running like mountain ranges across a landscape of wrinkled, spotted skin. Yet I could picture them hefting a 90-millimeter shell into the breach of a massive anti-aircraft gun, doing their part.

I glanced around the table. Others were nodding and I imagined them silently agreeing that even under the best of conditions war is hell.

"Okay," Tom interjected. "So much for the facts. Now tell him the other stories."

A sly grin crossed Mac's face. "What stories?" he asked innocently.

"Don't give me that malarkey. You know what stories."

"Oh. You mean like the time we were coming ashore on Saipan. We were in an open, flat-bottom landing craft and carrying a load of large steel plates. The seas were rough and we were taking on water and in danger of swamping the boat. The captain gave the order to ditch the cargo so we started lifting those plates and throwing them overboard. Unfortunately, the last plate we pulled up was actually the bottom of the boat. The water rushed in and we all drowned." He did an admirable job of keeping a straight face as he said this.

"Wait," I said. "You all drowned?"

"Yep."

It was my turn to smile. "That's pretty amazing. You drowned and lived to tell about it. What are the chances?"

"Probable … but not likely," Mac replied.

I stumbled on that one. "Probable but not likely? Is that even possible?"

He thought about that for a second. "Probably."

At that point Doc stepped in, perhaps to put our derailed conversation back on track. "Was that the one that won the award?" he asked.

"No, that was the one about the mosquitos." Mac looked directly at me. "You see, we were always short on medical supplies, especially blood. Well, the mosquitos on Tinian were really big and one enterprising young corpsman realized that if someone needed blood you could just grab one of those mosquitos, jab the proboscis in the patient's arm and squeeze until his face turned the right color. Worked every time."

# The Perpetual Order of Old People

Faces lit up around the table. No doubt this was another story they had heard before but enjoyed hearing again.

"And what award was that?" I asked.

"Second Biggest Liar in the United States, as declared by the Reliable Liar's Club. That was back in 1958." He seemed very proud of that dubious honor.

"So there's a club for liars?"

"Would I lie to you?" he asked, again with that sly grin.

I laughed while wondering if someone who lied about being a liar was actually telling the truth.

It had been a good day so far. People seemed entertained by Mac's stories and I felt pleased with having been a catalyst in that process. Things changed though when I spotted Doc. His expression was downcast, his lips drawn together and his eyes caught somewhere between despair and submission as he looked toward the center of the food court. I turned in that direction and saw a young man of Asian descent facing us from a short distance away. He stood proud and strong, like a statue of an ancient warrior, but whatever handsome features he might otherwise have possessed were lost to the contemptuous look on his face. His eyes, cold and accusing, shifted from one person at our table to the next, staying longer when they came to me. I nodded slightly while maintaining eye contact but he did not respond. Eventually, he turned and walked away. A few of us watched as he disappeared into the crowd. The rest just waited for someone to break the silence.

"Friend of yours?" I asked.

"We wish," Doc replied. "He works at Pagoda, across the way." Doc tilted his head in the direction of a Japanese restaurant on the opposite side of the food court. "I think he might be a manager there. That little show of defiance you just witnessed has been going on for about a year now. He's angry about something but … darned if I know what." Doc heaved a sigh and shook his head solemnly. "We call him Samurai."

"More like Sam *Awry*," Gus grumbled, though loud enough for everyone to hear. He ran a large, square hand over the stubble on his jaw.

The reference sounded appropriate. "Awry? As in off course?"

Tom nodded. "As in his life has gone off course and he blames us."

I turned back to the food court. Sam was long gone. "Take it he's not the talkative type."

"He spoke once," Dent said. "Came right up to our table and told us we don't belong here."

That surprised me. "You don't belong here?"

Dent shrugged. "That's what he said."

"Then what happened?"

"Harris faced him down."

I looked over at Harris, who after a second allowed himself to smile also.

# The Perpetual Order of Old People

Dent continued. "Harris suggested they take the discussion outside. Then he took his jacket off." With that Dent turned to Harris. "Go ahead. Show him. Take off your jacket."

"Guys, do I hafta?" Harris replied, though he had already started to stand. He slipped off the jacket and let it drop to his chair.

I haven't seen shoulders like that in a long time and those belonged to a college half-back. Bulging muscles on a broad chest stretched the fabric of his tee-shirt, and the flag tattooed on his bicep waved when he made and released a fist.

"Seventy-two years old and he's still intimidating," Doc observed. "Thankfully that potential altercation ended in a stare-down."

Harris did a short bow, put his jacket on and sat.

"Anyway," Doc continued, "Samurai still feels the need to express his animosity on occasion. He'll show up here, as he did today, to make sure we know he's watching. And a word of advice ... if you encounter him while walking through the mall just step to the side and let him pass. It's not worth escalating the situation. I don't know what's troubling him and can only hope that he gets past it someday."

"Don't hold your breath," Gus remarked.

It sounded to me like good advice.

# Chapter 6

It became part of my daily routine: arrive early, do my laps and grab a coffee before joining the group at their table. A voice kept saying *"you're leaving soon, this is temporary, don't get attached"* … but the camaraderie left me feeling younger, enthusiastic and eager to hear more stories. Roadwork forced a detour today that put me behind schedule and I rushed to squeeze in my workout before finding a seat.

"You look winded," Doc said.

I clutched my chest and feigned several labored breaths. "Is it that obvious? I'm trying to stick to my exercise regime and not miss any of your tales. Need to get my walk in before the mall gets too crowded."

"Ever consider joining a health club?" he asked.

A slow, confident nod. "I checked one out once but it looked more like perspiration prison. A lot of people sweating away, chained by headphones or glued to big-screen TVs, each of them locked in their own little world and oblivious to those around them. A lot of calories burned in a short amount of time perhaps but it certainly didn't seem relaxing. I left there convinced that the cost of a membership would not buy me the bliss I find in my solitary walks."

Harris reached to the center of the table and pointed an open box of donut holes in my direction. "Care to indulge? Might give you something to burn off later."

# The Perpetual Order of Old People

I waved a no-thanks. "It's hard enough without the temptation."

"I'll take one," Dent said from the far end of the table.

Harris picked up a sugar-coated morsel and lobbed it high in the air in Dent's direction. It missed the target, bounced off the table, landed on the floor and rolled under a nearby chair. Dent's eyes followed the wayward treat until it came to a stop.

"Five-second rule," Harris said, a proclamation that earned him a disapproving sideways glance from Doc.

Harris merely shrugged. "If you're willing to lick the floor for five seconds then you're welcome to eat anything that falls on it."

Dent waited, perhaps to see if any other regulations and guidelines regarding food dropped on the floor were forthcoming, then reached under the chair with his foot and putted the donut hole back into the open. He retrieved it and dropped it into his empty coffee cup. Game over.

I took a sip of my coffee. "So, where did we leave off? So far we've been to Normandy, Tinian, and Okinawa. Anyone else?"

Tom turned to the fellow sitting next to him, someone I'd seen before but couldn't put a name to the face. It was a memorable face though, movie-star looks with a square chin, a healthy head of neatly combed hair and eyes filled with confidence. "Your brother was on Okinawa, wasn't he?" Tom asked.

# Jeff Russell

A quick nod and wave in my direction invited me into the conversation. "Hi, I'm John by the way. Yes, my brother Bill was there back in October of '45 – after Japan surrendered – though his arrival was a bit unconventional. He was in the Navy and his ship, along with many others, was anchored off-shore. That's when Typhoon Louise struck. I don't think anyone expected it to be that bad. Some of those ships sank and others were washed ashore. Bill was lucky, his ship went aground and he got off safely."

John shook his head slowly at that point. "Others from his crew weren't so lucky. Their ship carried munitions, including dry powder bags that had to be offloaded. The powder in those bags gave off some form of gas that collected in the holds and five of the guys sent in to start the offload died from the fumes. That's really sad … you survive the war, you survive getting beached in a typhoon and then die from something so routine."

"But your brother was okay?" I asked.

"Sure, he did fine. Strange thing happened though. He was walking up and down the beach, looking to see where he might help, when he heard a voice he recognized. Turned out to be a friend from high school. After graduation, they went their separate ways, ended up in the Navy and then both get washed ashore on the same beach of some far-flung island."

"Guess the world isn't so big a place after all," I said.

# The Perpetual Order of Old People

"Guess not … not when war brings you together for a common purpose."

I took a moment to reflect on that observation before changing the subject. "And how about you? Any interesting sagas?"

John relaxed into his chair. "I spent my early years driving for the Flying Eagle Bus Company. It was mostly fixed routes between New York City and Hartford but now and then I'd take performers on the road. Seen Kansas, Denver, Colorado and California … all places I would never have had the chance to visit otherwise. Once I was assigned to shuttle a popular jazz group, Clarinet Jones and the High Notes, between Harlem and various venues in the northeast, some as far away as Boston. We made a lot of trips back and forth and one day I asked Clarinet why they just didn't stay overnight since many of their gigs were in the same part of the state. He asked me 'What color am I?' and I replied 'You're black.' He smiled then and said 'Blacks can't stay in most hotels here.' I didn't know that and it surprised me. Wasn't fair."

"No, it wasn't," I remarked. "Not by any standard."

John shook his head as if shaking off an unpleasant memory. "I had another assignment to drive Pete Delson – he was a big-time television talk-show host back in the day – and his entourage from New York to their studio out west. Pete was a really nice guy, regular people as we would say. He'd come up to the front of the bus and we would chat for hours during some of the long hauls.

# Jeff Russell

As part of my uniform, I wore a leather jacket with the bus company logo on it. Well … Pete liked that jacket so I jokingly offered to trade for his and he agreed. We swapped jackets and I gave his to my father. Dad was a big fan of Delson's show. He would sit in the living room, watch him on TV and say 'Hey Pete, I've got your jacket!' He was really proud of that." A heartwarming smile crossed John's lips.

"Good things come to those who ask," I noted. "Must have been an interesting job … driving celebrities around the country. Any mishaps along the way?"

His eyes looked back in time and he nodded. "One close call. I was driving – think it was in West Virginia, headed for Cincinnati – at a time when the interstate highway system was still under construction. Mountaintops had been pushed into valleys to make roadways and, honestly, none of it was very stable. Fortunately, the roads were all concrete and they lit up well under the headlights on a clear night. Around two in the morning I spotted a dark patch up ahead and stopped the bus. Turns out an entire slab of our lane had collapsed down the hillside. So I had to make a choice: either turn around and go back or risk going ahead. I got everyone off the bus and had them walk in the opposite lane, past the missing roadway, then followed by myself in the bus. Must have hit eighty miles an hour trying to get across as fast as I could but I made it. Later several people told me they could hear the gravel giving away under the weight of the bus. We hit the next town by daybreak and reported the situation to the local police. Kinda scary when you think about it … if the bus had continued in that same lane we would have gone down the hillside. Who knows how long it would have been before someone found us."

"So you've seen a lot from behind the wheel," I noted.

His head dipped slowly and rose again in a protracted, reaffirming nod. "That is true. I've had the pleasure and privilege of touring this country from coast to coast as it recovered from the war years and evolved into the land of opportunity. And I've seen firsthand what people can do when they set their mind to it. Pete Delson pushed himself to the top of the ratings and Clarinet Jones became a star because he never stopped believing that cool jazz and warm smiles could break down barriers. I owe a lot to that example. It inspired me to keep moving, to branch out and form my own company."

"And did you?"

"I did! Course that was a while ago. I'm retired now but still keep my fingers on the pulse of a thriving business that I built with my own hands. I'm proud of what I've accomplished but I also give credit where credit is due and as I see it the credit goes to those who inspire us to keep moving down the road, searching for something better."

Harris started clapping, and when we looked in his direction he added a broad grin. "Enough of the theatrics," he said. "Now tell him about your boat."

John's smile was a mix of modesty and pride as he removed a photo from his wallet and handed it over to me.

"He built that boat himself," Harris added.

It was a beautiful craft, a small yacht – if a forty-plus foot waterline could be considered small – with a full bridge above the main cabin. An elevated walkway extended from the bridge to the stern, forming a shelter over the rear deck, and the towering radar mast and antennae gave the vessel a majestic look. The name *Caryl K* appeared on the deckhouse just below the bridge. Having no personal experience in the trade I would have guessed this to be the work of many shipwrights laboring for months – even years – in a factory dedicated to producing pleasure craft for wealthy customers.

"You built this yourself?" I asked.

John nodded. "Along with some friends from my company. Took eighteen years to complete. Assembled the frame for the hull upside down in my shop so we could coat it with fiberglass. The glass fibers had to be laid over the hull and then the resin painted on and squeezed between the fibers. That took the longest time. Once the hull was finished we rolled it outside and had a crane flip it right-side up, then pushed it back into the shop. The superstructure was built separately; we couldn't attach that until she was ready to go in the water because otherwise, she wouldn't clear the bridges on the highway. Even going on the road turned out to be a challenge. I hired a company to tow the boat but they said that if they put my boat on their trailer the keel would not clear the hump at the end of my driveway. They didn't want to risk damaging the keel so they installed hydraulic jacks on the back of the trailer to lift the stern as she moved over that hump. Their foreman told me later that they used that trailer for other similar jobs so I guess it was a good idea."

"You must really like boats." I was stating the obvious but could see how the discussion brightened his eyes and wanted to keep it going.

"I do. I love to sail them, and I even love to maintain them … but most of all I love to build them. Boats are special. There is nothing you can ignore or short-change on a well-built boat, not if you want it to stay afloat at least. Every component is essential. It's like marriage in that respect."

His analogy was lost on me. "How so?"

He stared back as if I missed the obvious. "There's nothing you can ignore in marriage, not if you want smooth sailing. Every request, every response, every helping hand or shoulder to cry on or occasion to celebrate, no matter how big or small warrants your full attention. Dedication and attention to detail are essential in a good marriage."

I hadn't heard it put that way before, or if I had then I wasn't paying attention.

"So … is that where *Caryl K* fits in?"

"My wife. And my inspiration. She stood beside me through a lot of big plans and lean years. She's the one who inspires me to keep moving down the road."

He seemed very proud of that tribute. Ford had his motorcar, Eiffel had his tower and Westinghouse had his company … lasting namesakes in the memory of the man. John had his yacht and named it after his wife.

"How did you meet?" I asked.

"Funny story there. I had a friend – Arnie Branford – and I was dating his sister. Well, Arnie wanted to take his girlfriend to a movie in New York City, a real fancy date, and his girlfriend told Arnie she would only go if he found a date for her co-worker so they could all go together. Arnie asked me, even though I was already dating his sister. I agreed and that's how I met Caryl. We've been married sixty-six years now."

With that, John took the photo back, looked at it again and smiled. "My greatest accomplishment." When I raised my eyebrows in curiosity he replied, "A long and happy marriage."

"At least you followed the traditional route," Vic noted.

John looked over and gave him a curious glance. "You think doing your friend a favor by dating a new girl while you're already dating his sister is traditional?"

# The Perpetual Order of Old People

"Close enough," Vic replied. "I met my wife through the mail."

If the intent was to surprise me then he succeeded. "Through the mail?"

What Vic lacked in hair he made up for in smile. He had a jovial, round face, a perfect Santa Claus face with a perpetual, inviting smile that said he was happy to talk to anyone, anytime. I immediately felt comfortable having him join the conversation.

Vic nodded. "Yep. My brother was a couple years behind me in school. One day he told a classmate that I was in the Air Force, stationed in Germany and she said she remembered me. When he suggested that the two of us write to each other she agreed on the condition that I write her first. Guess she didn't want to seem too forward. He sent me her address and, since it was Christmas time and I didn't know what to write, I sent her a German Christmas card. She wrote back and that started our through-the-mail relationship. When I came home I called her and asked for a date. She agreed, but when I arrived to pick her up I learned that our 'date' would be at their dining room table, with her mother. So the three of us sat there and talked ... actually had a pretty good time, as first dates go. We continued dating after that and now we've been married fifty-two years."

"And what brought you to Germany?" I asked.

"I was in an Air Traffic Control Squadron, part of the Tactical Air Command supporting the fighter groups."

This was a direction we hadn't gone before and a chance for me to broaden my horizons. "Any interesting adventures to share?"

Vic's smile brightened a notch. "Well, getting there was an experience. We flew out of Floyd Bennet Field, in Brooklyn, with a refueling stop planned for the Azores. About two hours out we lost an engine – oil seal failure if I remember correctly. The plane was a Connie and …"

Vic's story went on but my mind had taken a detour. One second I was listening to him, caught up in the exploit, and the next second I was somewhere in the past, a darker place filled with regret with no idea how I'd gotten there. A quick rewind brought me back to something he said. *'The plane was a Connie.'* It took me another second to shake it off and return to the present.

"I'm sorry. What kind of plane?"

He paused mid-sentence to consider my question. "A Connie. A Lockheed C-121 Constellation, the big transport with four prop engines and three tail fins."

I could picture the plane but my recollection only went back to the civilian version used by commercial airlines. "Okay, I remember … the type TWA flew, right?"

"Yes, that's the one. They were small by today's standard but back then it seemed like an ocean liner with wings." He looked me in the eyes to see if I was still with him. I smiled an apology and nodded. His Connie was part of aeronautical history … my Connie was something altogether different.

"Anyway," he continued, "the pilot balanced the thrust between the remaining three engines, turned the plane around and headed back to the States. By this time we'd been flying in a thick fog for hours and it wasn't getting better. I guess there was some concern about making it home so we changed course and headed for a SAC base in Newfoundland. Then the pilot came on the intercom to tell us we might have to ditch in the ocean and instructed us to get into crash position. The Flight Sergeant broke us into groups and reviewed the procedure for kicking out the windows, climbing out on the wings and breaking out the life rafts. So we sat there, eyes wide open, waiting to see what would happen. Next thing you know the landing gear goes down and we made a bumpy but otherwise dry landing on the SAC airfield."

I tried to imagine myself caught in that scenario: staring out the window with nothing to see, losing altitude with no idea of what waited below, a jolting impact when we hit the water, crawling out a tiny window, trying to stand on the slick aluminum surface of a wing as the plane bobbed in heavy seas, waves crashing over my feet and everyone yelling at once but their voices muffled by a howling wind. It was not somewhere I'd ever want to be.

"Don't think I'd care to ditch in the North Atlantic," I said. "Were you scared?"

Vic shook his head. "Not at all. I was eighteen and just starting on my adventure. You don't think about death at eighteen."

I hadn't thought about death at that age either, but then again no one ever told me our plane was going to ditch in a foggy North Atlantic.

"So did you head back to the States after that?"

"No. We stayed at the SAC base until a replacement plane arrived and then flew straight to Germany, skipping the stop in the Azores. They told us the pilot had a date."

Vic smiled again at that point. I'm not sure he believed the bit about the pilot's date but it made a great ending to the story. I tried to sum things up as best I could. "So after a rather harrowing first step, you did a tour of duty in Germany, which led to a Christmas card, which led to a fifty-plus year relationship. Not what you might expect."

"Perhaps," Vic replied. "But I'm sure glad I followed my instinct. Sometimes you find the greatest treasures in unexpected places."

My eyes shifted back and forth between John and Vic. "Okay guys," I said. "What's your secret to a long and happy marriage?"

Mac raised his hand. "I can answer that one. Those three magic words. *Honey, I'm sorry*." More than a few guys laughed.

"And be part of each other's lives," Doc advised. "Do things together, go places together."

# The Perpetual Order of Old People

"I took my wife to a costume party once," Harris said. "I went as the Greek god Prometheus." He turned his head to the side, cocked his arm, pointed a clenched fist toward his forehead and made a face worthy of a deity.

"And your wife?" I asked.

"She went as the goddess Promiscuous."

I cringed. "Wait ... Prometheus and Promiscuous? Really?"

"You bet!" he replied. "We were one hot couple."

"I'm sure you were," Doc said. "Okay gents, that's it for me today. I have chores waiting. See everyone tomorrow."

I stood with Doc. "Yeah, I should head off also. They're talking snow later this morning and I want to get back before the driving gets tricky."

"Nothing to worry about," Mac said. "A dusting to a foot." Again he had that twinkle in his eyes.

"Dusting to a foot, huh? Guess that narrows it down. Any other details we should know about?"

"Sure, they're also predicting scattered darkness toward nightfall."

I gave up at that point. "Okay, good to know. Thanks, Mac."

"Ask me anything," he replied. "I'm a wealth of worthless information."

My hands went up to deflect the offer. "No thanks, I think I've had enough for now."

Mac waved me off with playful haughtiness. "You *think*? Ah … thinking is for amateurs. Tonight I'm going to sit down in a nice comfortable chair and contemplate the *un*thinkable."

I needed a moment to decipher that. "So … you're going to think about things that you can't think about. Do I have that right?"

He scrunched his face, rolled his eyes upward momentarily and then came back to me. "I think so."

At that point, Harris stepped in to break the deadlock. "A foot of snow ain't nothing," he said. "I seen two yards of snow once."

This time my eyebrows went up. "Two yards?"

"Yep. Front yard and backyard. Didn't bother shoveling either of 'em." He grinned and glanced toward Mac, I suppose to see if the volley would continue.

Mac shook his head. "Don't believe him," he said to me. "Next he'll be telling you that hamburgers aren't made out of ham."

Half the group moaned collectively and then one by one they stood to take their leave. Without further fanfare or foolery, the meeting was adjourned.

"Drive safe, everyone," Tom advised.

Temptation got the better of me and I opted to do a couple more laps on the off chance that Mac's predicted dusting came closer to two yards and kept me housebound for the next day or so. I also wanted to savor the experience of today's get-together while the images were still fresh. John's traveling adventures, Vic's first date with his future wife, even Harris's costume party were stories about people having fun. My life, in comparison, was a string of worthy accomplishments that looked good on a resume but were otherwise boring. Fun was never part of the equation and I began to wonder why. Had I somehow missed out on the lighter side of life? Had things gone so perfectly to plan that there were no humorous mishaps to retell? Or had they been there all along and I ignored them, brushing them off as irrelevant and letting them be swept into the dustbin of time. A quick review of the past fifty years was in order, the pursuit of some entertaining tidbit that I could share when we next met for coffee. My noble quest to recall some embarrassing misfortune was cut short when I spotted Samurai heading in my direction.

Doc's advice to steer clear of a potential incident seemed completely reasonable … and completely boring. I maintained course, waiting to see how the adversary would react. He continued coming straight at me. When we were about three feet apart I stopped, as did he. We studied each other, eyes locked in an adamant test of wills, each person silently claiming the right of way. I'll admit to being impressed. Up close his face was an artwork of angular features and proud imperial demeanor. Normally I give high marks for honorable behavior and while it was too early to tell if his intent was honorable I at least gave him credit for standing his ground. I smiled just enough to express an amusing interest in our little competition but he remained motionless, the undefeatable warrior statue with the grim face and dark, calculating eyes. When the game got tiresome I ceded him the first piece and stepped to the side, letting him pass. He did so without speaking and continued on his way.

# The Perpetual Order of Old People

## Chapter 7

At one time the flashing light on my answering machine had been a beacon of hope, the herald of good news regarding a contract or client, but lately, any calls to my home phone are either a wrong number, a sales pitch or updates regarding my planned relocation to Phoenix … a topic I was not always ready to tackle. After a moment's hesitation, I hit the play button.

*"Hi Uncle Jack, it's Molly! Cabern Ventures is really excited to meet you and they want to do an on-site interview. I hope this is not too soon but I've scheduled it for next week. I have your plane, rental car and hotel reservations booked and will email you the details. Can't wait to see you again! Bye!"*

The urge to protest faded in a heavy sigh. If her non-profit really wanted me onboard then an in-person interview would be necessary and Molly's enthusiastic intervention merely saved me the trouble of making the arrangements. All I have to do is show up on time and pay for everything. I decided, however, not to return her call until I was in a better mood to 'thank' her for taking the initiative.

The second message was from my real-estate agent, letting me know that another buyer was interested in my house and wanted to view it the following morning. I called her back to confirm that the property would be available and presentable for their tour.

# Jeff Russell

In retrospect, it has always been too much house for one person. My little mansion, which sits on three acres at the end of a cul-de-sac, boasts four bedrooms, three baths, and a two-car garage. Two of those bedrooms and the associated walk-in closets have been empty since the day I moved in six years ago. Another bedroom served as my now defunct home office. The dining room has a seven-piece furniture set covered with sheets to keep it dust-free, the bookshelf holds an impressive collection of works that no one else has ever perused and the kitchen has a massive granite island where I eat most of my meals.

Stepping outdoors one can see that the rest of the property is equally beautiful and equally idle. The front yard is large enough to accommodate an extravagant garden party but seldom has visitors other than the crew that mows the lawn, the backyard has room for an elaborate swing set but currently is home only to my hammock, and the stone patio has a top-of-the-line grill that has never cooked more than one burger at a time. I purchased the house believing it fit my image – stately and successful – but in reality, it underscores my status in life … lonely.

The rest of the day was spent doing my own walk-thru: uncovering furniture, making sure that tables were clear, shelves were neat, personal items were stored away and the kitchen was tidy. The jigsaw puzzle and chess set would stay put, as they are testaments to my unending quest for scholarly endeavors and with any

# The Perpetual Order of Old People

luck, the potential buyer would move a piece and make my life more interesting.

It occurred to me, as I prepared for bed, that I had lived a relatively sheltered life. No picnic, to be sure, but my challenges were limited to rising in rank and staying ahead of the crowd. Decades of that could not compare to the months others spent in actual combat – where each day was a struggle to stay alive. Perhaps I was naïve, or perhaps it was because I had the luxury of picking my own battles, but for whatever reason, I was always confident of that next promotion and next big contract. Success was a given and risk, what little I faced, was always acceptable. Not so for others, those who put their life on the line every time they went to sea or stormed a beach or held a position against an advancing enemy. For them, risk was a matter of life and death and success was something you didn't plan on. My accomplishments were measured on a balance sheet; theirs were measured from the deck of a landing craft to whatever protection they found on an enemy-held beach. Keeping my head above water meant paying my bills on time; keeping theirs above water was do or die. My career was over and I was still young for my age; they aged a lifetime before turning twenty.

Some men are scarred by their experiences, and some – the unlucky ones – are broken. But there are others who trekked through hell and came back strong enough to face each new day and wise enough to appreciate everything and everyone around them. I sat there wondering how I would have fared if forced to risk it all, only to realize that – not long ago – I was in that very situation and did not fare well.

# Chapter 8

I'd driven through Stamford on several occasions over the past couple years, always on the interstate, always glancing to the right, to the fourth floor of the tallest building in this part of the city's skyline, always wondering what would have happened if I hadn't called things off. Today I took the exit ramp and battled the noontime traffic while making my way to a municipal parking garage. A one-block walk and a quick elevator ride brought me to the lobby of Carlton-Fisher Marketing. Throughout the morning I remained resolute, determined to see this through but as I stood there facing the receptionist I wondered again whether coming here was a mistake. Sometimes the past should remain in the past, old wounds should be left to heal and memories left to fade. Unfortunately some memories refuse to die; instead, they return to haunt us with the darkening, weighing, constricting anguish of regret. And sometimes dealing with that regret means returning to the scene of the crime in the hope of making a better memory. That was my mission today.

"Can I help you, sir?" the receptionist asked.

I didn't recognize her. The previous receptionist, the one from two years ago, knew me well and always buzzed Connie when I arrived. But now I was an unknown, a stranger who showed up unannounced in the hope of having lunch with the vice-president. Suddenly my plan seemed foolish, rushed and unprofessional. For all I knew Connie had moved on – another position with another firm in another big city – and left the past in the past. There was only one way to find out.

"Connie Pendleton, please."

The receptionist scanned her computer and then looked up at me. Her stare was insinuating and I felt like a salesman on a cold call trying to catch a senior executive between meetings. For a second my years of confidence, of command and control, abandoned me. Then I shook it off.

"Tell her it's Jack Brouder." I hoped it sounded more assertive than it felt.

She continued to stare but then shifted her eyes to the side, off to my left, before coming back to me. When I turned around Connie was standing there.

"I didn't expect to see you here," she said.

The fear of commitment that plagued my past must have blinded me at the time, for she was even more beautiful than I recalled: tall, slender and radiant, platinum-blonde hair curling at the shoulders, aqua-marine eyes at once dazzling and intellectual, and delicate lips that could deliver a spellbinding business proposal. We met when Carlton-Fisher took over marketing for a small firm with a good product that was going nowhere. I came onboard to tackle their logistics issues and she and I worked together at the client site for several months. Meetings became lunches, lunches became dinners and eventually, we were spending our nights together even though she was ten years younger than me and infinitely more appealing. Our courtship continued after the job ended but when she proposed taking things to the next level I backed away. Some unpleasant discussions followed and we haven't spoken since.

"I was hoping we could have lunch," I replied.

Those dazzling, intellectual eyes could also be piercing and steely, an intense focus that locked her target in the crosshairs. I hadn't forgotten that look and recognized it now. She held me prisoner for several long seconds.

Her head turned slightly toward the receptionist while her eyes remained fixed on me. "Penny, bump my one o'clock to one-thirty." Then she faced me again. "We'll have to make this quick."

The café was crowded and noisy. I would have preferred an intimate setting but the clock was ticking with little hope of getting another chance. To make things worse I'd forgotten my lines. What I needed to say sat jumbled on my tongue and I couldn't decide where or how to begin.

Waiting was never Connie's strong suit. "I'm seeing someone," she said. "And it's serious." Her tone was cold and blunt as if the words were meant to strike the final blow in the opening round.

"Well, I'm glad to hear that," I replied, though a part of me felt it wasn't quite true. She was special and if I hadn't been so myopic, so afraid of what a serious relationship might have cost me I would have seen that earlier. We could have been something special together.

"You deserve someone," I told her. "You deserve … more than I offered."

My confession went unacknowledged. She continued to watch me, stone-faced, sitting with her back straight and her hands folded on the table. It was her inflexible, condescending pose. I'd seen it before.

"What's this all about?" she asked.

*Honey, I'm sorry.* I swallowed hard. "I owe you an apology. We bordered on something in the past, a commitment, a big one actually, and I wasn't prepared for it. A move like that takes guts and I didn't have what it takes. You did … you had as much invested and as much to lose and still you were willing to put everything on the line for me. But I wasn't … and I'm very, very sorry for that."

She hadn't moved, hadn't relaxed her shoulders or loosened the grip of her stare but I heard her exhale, long and slow as if letting go of the breath she'd been holding.

"I just wanted to tell you that, tell you that you were right, before I left."

As we sat there – hers eyes still defensive, mine remorseful – I could read her mind. '*Fine. We're done here. Good riddance.*' It was not how I wanted this to end but it was what I deserved. At least I accomplished what I set out to do. Neither of us had touched our meal and I imagined that we would part then and there. I would pay the bill, leave the tip and walk away hoping she despised me a little less than the last time we talked.

"Where are you going?"

The question surprised me, or maybe it was the voice behind the question, softer than before with what sounded like a hint of genuine interest. And her eyes were different. They were open a bit wider, the arc of her eyebrows slightly relaxed. She wasn't smiling but the slight curve to her lips reminded me that, back then at least, her laugh could light up the room.

"Out West. To be with what's left of my family."

She looked down and to the right, something she did when deep in thought, and then came back to me. "Your niece?"

I nodded gratefully. "Molly, yes. And my nephew, plus his wife and their kids."

The satisfaction of having been right flickered in her eyes. "And how is Molly? Still single?"

Another nod. "I think she takes after her mom, going slow to enjoy life at each stage. Karen married in her mid-twenties, then waited five years before having Connor and another five before having Molly."

"So that makes Molly what ... twenty-five now?"

The best I could offer was a shrug. "Something like that. It changes every year. I can't keep track."

Connie had this uncanny ability to go long stretches without blinking. I never asked whether she was so engrossed in whatever was being discussed that blinking would have risked missing something ... or if it was intentional, her way of maintaining dominance in a conversation. I'd forgotten all about that until just now, when she blinked.

She smiled then, for real. Not a sinister or patronizing smile but an understanding, if not '*I told you so*' smile. "So you finally decided you need a family."

I ventured a smile of my own but kept it sheepish. "More like recognized. I've always had the people around me – my military and business associates – to keep me company. Someone was always there, close enough to talk when I needed to chat yet not close enough to threaten my personal space. But now I'm retired and all that has gone away, the camaraderie and companionship I depended on for all those years but failed to appreciate."

"Man was not meant to be alone," she said.

A laugh, or at least the shadow of a laugh, a quick breath with no vocals slipped out before I could stop it. "I know … you told me that once, more than once actually, and you were right. You were so right about us … about everything."

People were not meant to be alone. Connie knew this better than I and for that reason, she had Mu – a magnificent black crow with feathers that shined as if they were oiled, ebony eyes that appeared to look every direction at once and a long, curved beak that remained closed when she held him but opened menacingly when I came near. We met during my first visit to Connie's place. "I adopted Mu while volunteering at an animal

# The Perpetual Order of Old People

hospital," she told me at the time. "He came in with a broken foot and I took him home to help him heal. We've been buddies since."

She was busy preparing dinner for him – dry cat food supplemented with a mixture of chopped pasta, pepperoni, string cheese, and corn. I'd seen other crows dining by the roadside and in comparison, this meal looked pretty good.

"*Mu* is his name?" I asked. "That's … unusual."

Connie nodded. "It's the twelfth letter of the ancient Greek alphabet, though nowadays it's also the metric prefix representing micro. Get it? *Micro … my crow?*"

I remembered laughing then and it made me smile now. It was a strange memory … one from the distant past, before our relationship capsized, and yet thinking back on it while sitting across from Connie here in the café made it feel like yesterday. I haven't felt that close to anyone in a very long time.

"Do you still have Mu?" I asked.

A smile slipped through her defense. "Yes, we're still there for each other. He sees me off every morning and welcomes me home at night."

"Not much of a conversationalist," I joked.

She laughed aloud. It was good to hear her laugh, even at my expense. "Are you still mad about that?"

"*Go-ay. Go-ay.*" I did my best to mimic a bird impersonating a human. "Go away … are you sure you didn't teach him that?"

She gave me a sly look and I wondered if my attempt to sound clever had backfired. At one point my conversations weren't all that rewarding either. "No, that one he learned on his own. He's a pretty good judge of character."

The barb hung in the air. I deserved it.

"You know," she then said, "sometimes a little conversation can go a long way … especially where love is involved."

Love. I've always been mystified, and perhaps a bit frightened by that word. Love was some strange magic that everyone talked about, as natural as breathing but foreign to me. It mandated a willingness to blindly hand over one's material and emotional wellbeing that I could not rationalize on paper. I have always prided myself on serving an essential role in some noble purpose but when it came to forming a permanent bond with another person, one that I could not simply walk away from, one where the risk of being hurt exceeded the perceived benefits because I never really understood what it meant to be in love … then I disappointed everyone … especially myself.

"I need to head back," Connie said. She reached her hand across the table, fingers outstretched, palm facing me.

My breath waited and my skin tingled with anticipation as my hand drew closer to hers. I'd forgotten that feeling, that prelude to a strange magic.

# The Perpetual Order of Old People

Then we locked hands, a simple gesture that once upon a time meant everything.

"Thanks for coming to see me, Jack. I'm glad we did this, glad this ended on a happier note. I hope things go well for you out west. And I'm sorry I called you an old fool … you're really not that old."

I wanted to ask *'But I'm still a fool?'* but held back. We both knew the answer to that one.

She smiled again, though I sensed a trace of sadness in her eyes, the acceptance that we had arrived at where we could have been, perhaps where we both wanted to be, only to find it was too late. That smile and the look in her eyes stayed with me for the rest of the day.

# Chapter 9

Morning brought a wintry mix that started as ice but transitioned to rain about the time I would normally leave for the mall. After some deliberation I grabbed my coat and headed off, determined to show up at the group table in case anyone else braved the elements. When I got there Tom was the only one present.

"We have a rule," he said after waving me over. "When the weather is bad everyone stays home. No sense taking chances. I show up to make sure that everyone obeys the rule."

I smiled. "Someone has to stand watch, right?"

"Right! He eyed me in mock annoyance and bounced his fist off the table. "I should put you on report for showing up today but since you're new I'll cut you a break. Plus I get lonely sitting here by myself."

I took a seat across from him.

"It is a little dicey out there," I commented. "Hope no one else ventures out."

"Gus will for sure," Tom noted. "He was hardcore Army. Not likely that a little foul weather will keep him from seeing Emma. He's a man on a mission."

The image of Gus as a teenager, charging ahead with rifle in hand, his teeth gritted and eyes burning with determination slowly changed to that of a grumpy old geezer stepping over a snowbank while holding a bouquet of flowers and smiling with anticipation.

"He must really love her," I noted.

# The Perpetual Order of Old People

Tom nodded. "He does, but love works both ways you know. She's his purpose in life, his reason to keep going, and that's something you don't want to lose. It's like that for most of us, actually. When you find that special someone your whole life takes on a new meaning. Doesn't matter what you've done before, how many beaches you've stormed or missions you flew or bullets you dodged. What matters is that you have a new objective in life – protecting and caring for someone else – and that makes life worth living, especially as we get older."

He paused, and I could tell by the look on his face that something troubled him.

"Course, it doesn't always work out," he continued. "There's risk and sacrifice involved with that level of commitment but I can't think of a truly worthwhile goal that doesn't involve risk and sacrifice."

Those words echoed in my mind – risk and sacrifice – two basics of a meaningful existence that were essentially missing from the story of my life. The risks I'd taken amounted to passing on one opportunity in favor of another and my sacrifices were more self-serving than patriotic or philanthropic. In the midst of this confession, I reached for my decaf ... only to realize that I hadn't gotten that far yet.

"I'm gonna grab a coffee. Can I get you a refill?"

Tom checked his cup; it was empty. "Thanks. Cream, no sugar."

# Jeff Russell

The intermission gave me a quiet moment to reflect. I advanced in rank, I landed the big contracts, I was financially secure with no strings attached and yet they – Doc, Vic, John, Mac and who knows who else – seemed happier. They fought tougher battles and got fewer breaks but still came out in front. Why? Clearly, in my quest to stay ahead of the crowd, I had overlooked what was obvious to everyone else. A significant someone? Probably. I filed that transgression away to revisit at a later time. For now, there was another matter I wanted to address, one that called for a private audience and today seemed like a prime opportunity.

"So what's Doc's story?" I asked after presenting Tom with his coffee. "He encourages others to speak up but his personal history remains a mystery."

Tom nodded slowly. I could sense he was choosing his words carefully. "There's a reason we call him 'Doc' … that was his job during the war. He had just started his pre-med program when duty called and he answered. The Army was short on medics and when they learned that he knew the difference between a flesh wound and a fracture they threw a field manual and first-aid kit at him and sent him to the front lines. He wasn't ready for it – said so himself – and I think the whole experience was a bit traumatic. Don't get me wrong, a lot of guys have him to thank for making it home. I know Doc is pleased with that but you can't save everybody … no one can save everybody … and he still carries the scars of every life that slipped away, still blames himself for failing them."

Tom took a cautious breath. "I probably shouldn't repeat this but he told me once that he used to tremble at the thought of not being able to save the next patient; that the fear of failing would keep him up at night. Then the next day he'd be back in a makeshift OR with no sleep and no confidence and praying that the injuries wouldn't be so severe that someone might die because he wasn't good enough at his job. That must be an awful load to bear."

His focus drifted away as he sipped his coffee.

"Anyway, after the war Doc went on to complete his degree. I think he did that because he didn't want the fear of failing again to follow him throughout his life. And it's lucky for the rest of us that he did; went on to become a fine surgeon. But he's still real private about the war years, they're not something he wants to relive. He calls us his support group and I think that seeing us, being with us reminds him that he did a lot of good back then. It helps to have those reminders. Some of the people he saved could be sitting around tables, having coffee with other vets right now because he was there back then."

I waited as Tom stared off into the distance. "I've seen a lot of that," he finally said. "Men who have a proud history trapped behind some horrendous memory. Men who played a vital role in keeping the world safe for democracy but can't deal with the fact that someone

– even the enemy, an enemy who was trying to kill them – died a horrible death because of something they did. Truth is, the men on the battlefield were simply men, everyday guys forced to go to war and just hoping to stay alive. Didn't matter what side you were on, you did your job and prayed you'd make it home again. But doing your job meant preventing someone else from doing theirs and usually, that meant killing them. For most humans, that's not an easy thing to do, and the closer you get, when you can see the pain in their eyes and the fear on their face, the harder it becomes. Watching someone agonize because you pulled the trigger first or had the better aim is not easy. It's hard to live with that and still feel human."

He took another sip of coffee. "For many of the vets I've talked to a few minutes of horror and the resulting guilt overshadows everything they accomplished during their years of service. For those men, the war remains private and we need to respect that."

I looked at Tom, admiring a side of him I hadn't expected. "That's a lot to carry around. Hope those men found someone to talk to about it."

He was still looking away and once again nodded. "Let's hope." Then he turned back to me. "Gus is another one, by the way. Purple Heart, but won't reveal the circumstances. There's something buried deep inside that tears at him but he doesn't want to let it out. Ask him a question and he clams up. Like I said … private."

# The Perpetual Order of Old People

After a pause, he adopted a slightly cheerful expression, though I couldn't tell if it was genuine or forced. "So how are the moving plans?" he asked.

I took the hint – time to change the subject. "Flying out in a few days for an interview. I think I mentioned that my niece is trying to fix me up with a non-profit looking for someone in my field. She told them I have the logistics experience they need. I'm not really excited about this but I think it's about time I hooked up with my family again. Suppose I mentioned that already also."

"As I recall you weren't too happy about it at the time," Tom replied. "Sure you want to do this? Sounds like a big step."

My head rocked slowly from side to side. It was an involuntary reflex, the body's way of killing time while the mind stares down the darkened path ahead.

"And it gets worse. I think Molly is planning to fix me up with a lady friend as if shipping me across the country and finding me a new job isn't enough." Normally I frown on sarcasm but today it felt justified.

"Why do you say that?"

"Oh, just something she said recently about me shopping around for someone special and knowing if they are the right one. The questions were innocent enough but they came out of the blue and I can't help but think she has something up her sleeve."

Tom looked me straight in the eye. "That's going *way* above and beyond. May be time to pull your hat out of the ring."

The best I could do was shake my head. "Could just be my imagination. Besides, I'm not serving a purpose here, and to be honest I miss that feeling. I've spent the past half-century knocking myself out for a paycheck and told myself that was long enough, that I could be happy leaving the rat race behind, but I didn't realize retirement would be this boring."

"Yes, well … that's where having a spouse comes in handy," Tom replied. His smile soon melted away. "Actually, to say *handy* doesn't do it justice. Parents serve a purpose when their kids are young but eventually, the kids move out. That can leave a hole in your life, the so-called *empty nest* thing. Having a spouse gives you a reason to keep going, to keep pushing yourself and personally I believe we all need that, need to feel important. Having a family is nice but for those of us lucky enough to still have a partner in life it means so much more."

His smile returned then. "Just make sure it's a partner you pick out and not one Molly finds for you."

I grinned and nodded to acknowledge his sage advice but inside I wondered if I'd ever have a significant someone to give my life purpose without some form of third-party intervention … divine or otherwise.

# The Perpetual Order of Old People

We sat there, lost in our individual thoughts until Tom sat upright and put on a fresh smile. "So ... what was your old job like?"

It's a strange feeling ... being proud and embarrassed at the same time. I did my best to adopt a professional glow. "The proverbial one-man show. I was chief cook and bottle washer for a company that provided specialized logistics solutions to medium and large sized corporations. They'd have a problem and I'd solve it, which typically meant finding a safe, fast and cost-effective strategy for moving their product or the raw material that went into it. Often it included items that were time-sensitive or required special-approval for handling – hazmat and that sort of thing. Once we had a plan I would integrate that with a shipping firm to manage the actual transport. Most jobs were one-and-done but several clients kept me on retainer, working with them during the development stage so that we'd have a logistics plan in place when the product went to market."

"Sounds interesting," Tom said.

I nodded. "It was ... and I enjoyed most of it: suit and tie, plans and procedures, flying here and there to meet with stakeholders of global corporations. It made me feel like I was playing a key role in something vital to the economy. Suppose I needed that as much for my ego as for my bottom line. But the truth is my own business wasn't as efficient as some of the solutions I devised for others. I was hanging on financially but working myself to death in the process. All along I had this vision of a beautiful office with a commanding view, a massive oak desk and a staff to help make the impossible possible. That was the dream ... but the older I got the less I expected it to come true. I was on the verge of giving it up when someone made an offer for the company. Suddenly my dream was this great leisurely retirement but, as I pointed out, in reality, it's not so great."

The conversation stalled as I debated whether to continue. "Spent the better part of my career shooting for that corner office, then worked my butt off when I started to worry that it wouldn't happen. Looking back I can't really say it was worth it."

Tom sat watching me, his expression a mix of compassion and understanding. No doubt he had a dream or two in his lifetime.

"And the new job?" he asked.

I put on my happy face. "Molly's non-profit. They buy old text books from school districts that are upgrading to a newer edition and resell them to other districts that have limited budgets, usually in other parts of the country. The books are still good, the content is generally still valid but perhaps a little out of date. For many school districts, however, that's good enough. I think I can help by streamlining the process, perhaps shipping directly from seller to buyer and skipping the interim warehouse storage, but I'd need to know more about their operation first. Just not sure I want to get that involved. The job ruled my life once and I think there are more important things to live for."

"Like family?" Tom asked. "That's a big commitment too."

I nodded. "Family would be nice. And who knows … maybe even a spouse someday!" I added a whimsical grin to hide my thoughts.

"I wish you luck," he replied. "For now we should both shove off. It's too dark outside for this time of morning and I think the weather's gonna get worse before it gets better."

"Thanks for the chat," I told him as we stood. "And thanks for not putting me on report."

Apparently, this *was* my lucky day, for after bidding farewell to Tom I spotted Samurai on my way to the parking garage. This time I had the tactical advantage – he hadn't seen me yet – and I used that opportunity to set a course clear of other shoppers. Soon I was in his sights and, while pretending to be distracted, watched from the corner of my eye as he came straight at me. When we were inches apart he stepped quickly into my lane and struck a glancing blow, his shoulder against mine. I'll confess to being surprised – I hadn't expected physical contact – and was even more surprised when he kept walking without looking back, as if nothing had happened … or worse yet as if I didn't matter.

## Chapter 10

Spring was in the air. The grass was covered in snow, the robins were still on vacation, the buds had not yet tinged the barren maple branches red and yet spring was definitely in the air. I could smell it, clean and refreshing, just cold enough to stimulate the senses like strong coffee did back when I could drink strong coffee. And I could see it in the way the brilliant morning sun reflected off every frosted surface between my house and the mall. It was a day that began like most winter days and yet today felt enchantingly different. A moment of introspection explained why … friends were waiting ahead. The void in my life had been filled. I banished the thought that moving to Phoenix would mean leaving them behind and quickened my pace.

Dent and Harris were chatting in line when I stepped up behind them. "The world would be a dark and dreary place," I said, "if there wasn't a coffee shop within arm's reach."

They turned around and we exchanged handshakes. "Amen to that. I'm Dent by the way … don't think we've been formally introduced."

Dent stood a head shorter than Harris. He had a slight build, a quasi-hippy haircut that finished in a short ponytail and a neatly trimmed salt-and-pepper goatee. His round, wire-rim glasses sat low on the bridge of his nose. The confidence in his voice and sureness in his eyes left the impression that what he lacked in brawn he made up for in brain. We continued to talk as Harris, a physically intimidating man with a gentle-giant expression and a regulation crewcut stepped forward to order his coffee.

"I've been meaning to ask … is *Dent* a first name, last name, nickname?"

He gave me an understanding smile. "Short for Denton, my grandmother's maiden name. My dad was in the auto repair business and thought that 'Denton Bender' had a nice ring to it."

The name triggered a fuzzy memory that I couldn't put in focus. "Why does that sound familiar?"

This time there was a touch of pride in his smile. "Probably from my commercials." We paused while getting our coffee and continued the discussion on the way back to the group table.

"I served in Nam for a couple years, starting in '65, working in the motor pool. Spent most of that time fixing up jeeps and trucks that had gotten blown to hell. After the war, I helped out at my dad's repair shop. I specialized in bodywork – to me there's something gratifying about making a banged-up car look new again – and he started introducing me to his clients as 'Dent Fenbender' because getting the dents out of the fenders was my job. When he retired I took over the business and changed the name to Dent Fenbender's Auto Repair. My radio and print commercials had the catch-line *'Bring your fender-bender to Dent FenBender.'* Corny, I suppose, but it worked. We had customers lined up out the door, so much so that I had to bring in help to do the engine and transmission work. That's when I met Harris – he's a genius when it comes to gears and pistons."

Harris raised his coffee cup to acknowledge the compliment. "Another motor pool graduate," he said. "Bumped into Dent at a VFW convention and he practically begged me to come work with him." He dipped his head slightly, raised his eyebrows and looked at Dent as if waiting for a retort.

Dent smirked. "I told him that if he had nothing better to do he was welcome to hang out at my shop, and that if he was careful I'd let him pick up a wrench now and then. Alas, you can't keep a good man down and, as I said, he was the best at what he did. I didn't want to swell his head by telling him that at the time but I made him a co-owner so he wouldn't go elsewhere."

"Rivalry and respect can make for a beautiful friendship," I said. "Do you two still work together?"

Harris shook his head. "Sadly, no. After too many years of bickering from sun up to sun down, we couldn't stand each other another day. We sold the business, split the profit and now face off on the tennis court. Dent's got no power in his swing but he can put the ball just where he wants it."

"Though maybe not for much longer," Dent confided. He wrapped his left hand around his right wrist. "A touch of arthritis … makes it hard to keep a grip on the racket when Harris fires his howitzer. I'm taking pain pills for it but those only do so much. Got a

# The Perpetual Order of Old People

meeting with my primary next week; hoping he can prescribe something stronger."

Mac had been listening to the conversation, his eyes bouncing between Dent and Harris like a ball sailing back and forth over the net as they traded zingers. "My cardiologist prescribed an anti-arithmetic for me," he said. "I take one pill every day."

Something didn't sound right with Mac's description. "Say again?"

"He means an antiarrhythmic," Doc explained. "To control his heartbeat."

"That's what I said," Mac continued. "An anti-arithmetic. It must be working because now I can't do simple math in my head. I can't even balance my checkbook."

At that point, Millie joined the discussion. "He can't balance the checkbook because I won't give it to him." She tossed her head sideways in his direction. "He's from the Perpetual Order of Perpetually Overdrawn."

The temptation was too much and I ventured a guess. "P-O-P-O. Poo-poo?"

Mac pouted defensively. "I can't be overdrawn … I still have some checks left!"

My eyes shifted back and forth between Mac and Millie while trying to decide if this conversation was for real. In the end, I took the safe route. "Better make sure he takes his meds," I told her. "And hide the checkbook."

"Hope we're not late."

That buoyant greeting came from a couple who approached the table and found seats alongside Tom at the far end. The gentleman looked around and then waved to me. "I'm Don and this is my wife Janie. We met earlier but haven't made it here lately. Tom called, said you might be leaving soon and suggested we stop by for a little show-and-tell." He held up a manila folder. "So I brought pictures."

"Don flew as a turret gunner in a TBF Avenger during the war," Tom explained. "He saw a lot of action in the South Pacific and I thought you'd enjoy hearing his stories."

I nodded my appreciation to Tom and then waved to the newcomers. "Hi, I'm Jack. Nice to meet you both again."

"Swap seats," Tom said while standing. "This way you won't have to shout back and forth."

Bodies shifted out of the way as Tom and I played musical chairs. "Okay, TBF Avenger … I recognize the name but the details are a little fuzzy."

Don withdrew a photograph from his folder and handed it over to me. It was an impressive shot of an Avenger in flight. Large and ungainly, it looked more like a workhorse than a thoroughbred.

"Hell of a good plane," he said. "Carrier-based, single engine, folding wings so we could fit more of them in the hanger deck. That large bay door underneath held a torpedo, though sometimes we carried bombs in there. Three crew members: pilot up front, bombardier in the middle and turret gunner facing aft. What you see here is the typical Navy color scheme: blue on top to blend in with the ocean when viewed from above and white on the bottom to blend in with the clouds when viewed from below."

The lines around his eyes appeared to fade as he spoke. "She saw action all throughout the Pacific, from Midway to Guadalcanal. And she has a history with famous personalities. George Samuelson, the senator, was an Avenger pilot before turning to politics and Paul Ratchford, the screen star, was a turret gunner before he went into acting."

Don had an accomplished, determined look about him and it made me wonder if certain roles in life prepare a man for greatness or if instead great men simply gravitate to those roles. I was drawn back to the conversation when he pointed out the tiny bubble at the rear of the canopy. "That was my station, the turret gun, like Tom said. It was a part-time gig – my rank was Aviation Machinist Mate First Class – but when I wasn't fixing planes I was squeezed into the turret seat, sitting alongside a big fifty-caliber and looking straight down the length of the barrel. It provided a great view of the target."

"Must have been a great view during take-off," I said. "Facing aft and watching the carrier fade into the distance as you climb into the clouds. Do you remember your first carrier launch?"

Don laughed. "Yes … but for all the wrong reasons. Back then the front landing gear struts were attached to the catapult and the tail wheel was chained to the deck with a link that broke at a predetermined tension. When the catapult fired, the plane was pinned in place until that link separated, sort of like stretching an elastic band until one end slips out of your fingers. The pilot came on the intercom beforehand and told us to fasten our seat harness but I didn't, figuring 'what the heck – I'm crammed in here – where can I go?' Turns out the only place to go was face-first into the trigger pod that aimed and fired the gun. I lost a few teeth and a lot of blood learning that lesson. A couple of hours later we were back onboard. I went to sick-bay and they fixed me up."

"Ouch," I replied. "Tough way to learn. Did the turret rotate?"

His demeanor brightened. "A hundred-twenty degrees to either side. And it was fast, electrically driven. You tell it to move and it moved quick."

He looked at the picture again and rocked his head slowly from side to side as if sweeping away the years. "This one time we were making a run on a Jap carrier and our approach took us straight between two escort destroyers. The pilot dropped down to wave top level and as we flew between those ships I kept swinging the turret from side to side, fast as I could, firing at anything I could hit. We were lucky the Japs didn't shoot back, probably out of fear of hitting each other."

# The Perpetual Order of Old People

Whatever youth he relived during his nostalgic trip back in time slipped away as he reached into the folder for another photo. "This one's not so pretty," he said.

The picture was a grainy black and white of an Avenger parked on a debris-covered surface. Someone could be seen running past, looking toward the plane, while another figure crouched beside a firehose and directed a stream of water at the engine cowling. A wall of smoke partially obscured other people laboring in the background.

"That was taken onboard the USS Cabot – a light carrier – CVL-28. She was on patrol off the Philippines at the time. We were sitting in the catapult, preparing to take off, when the ship was attacked by a flight of kamikazes. One came in from aft and flew directly over us, inverted. He had already been hit – his plane was on fire – but he kept coming and I caught a glimpse of the pilot's face before he crashed into the deck directly in front of us. I was strapped into my seat and couldn't turn around but I heard the explosion, even over the roar of our own engine, and saw a bright flash followed by a mountain of black smoke. Flying debris sheared off our prop but … miraculously … none of us were hurt. We scrambled out just before that picture was taken."

My eyes went wide as he spoke. "Wait … you were on that plane when it got hit? That very plane?"

Don nodded slowly. The relief I expected to see on his face wasn't there. "We were lucky, others weren't. The explosion blew off several of the catwalk gun tubs, along with their crews. It also took out the catapult – the only one we had – and killed several crew members near and around our plane. We were in the center of the blast but somehow survived."

Jan laid her hand on Don's as he stared at the photo. She had warm, sympathetic eyes that said *burdens are easier when you share them.*

"That was the second kamikaze hit we took that day," Don continued. "The other plane crashed into our port side, exploding in the hanger deck. A lot of guys died that day." He pursed his lips and slowly rocked his head.

"But the Cabot kept fighting. Two direct hits couldn't sink her, she kept fighting until the attack was over. We sailed into a squall, with repair ships lashed port and starboard, and stayed there until repairs were made. Then we returned to combat."

He took the photo back, looked at it again for several seconds and returned it to the folder.

I could see how the memory weighed on him. "Pretty traumatic duty, I imagine."

"Yes, much of it. But there were fun times too, like when they let me help pick out replacement aircraft."

"What was that about?"

"The Navy stationed replacement aircraft – some new, others repaired – on a small atoll that had a runway and a tent to house the Army sentry assigned to guard the place. Whenever we lost planes in battle I would fly out to the atoll, along with some pilots. We'd inspect the planes, choose those we wanted to replenish our squadron and then fly them back to the Cabot. Being the mechanic meant I did the inspection. I would do a visual on the outside and then climb into the cockpit and taxi to the runway to test the engine, brakes and control surfaces. Other pilots would do the same and often we'd have two planes lined up side-by-side on the runway, wings folded back and engines revving. Next thing you know we'd be drag racing down the runway and back, sometimes hitting a hundred miles an hour and with the tail wheel off the ground. I'm sure the Army sentry thought we were nuts!"

"Making the best of a tough time I suppose."

"Mixing pleasure with business," Don replied.

"So tell me … how did you two meet?"

The change of subject prompted a cheerful smile on Jan's part. "We were high school sweethearts," she said.

Don smiled back. "Always figured we'd get married someday but the war got in the way. I enlisted in the Navy in July of '42 and was sent to boot camp in Newport, Rhode Island. It was an abbreviated version because the Navy needed people right away. After that, I went to gunnery school in Quonset, Rhode Island, received aircraft training in Groton, Connecticut, and then reported to the USS Santee. She was newly commissioned; started out as an Esso oiler but the Navy converted her into an aircraft carrier. We departed Norfolk and headed east to participate in the North

Africa campaign. I flew a lot of missions out of there … even still have my log books."

"They turned an oil tanker into an aircraft carrier?"

Don nodded. "It was a natural choice. Tankers have a lot of space below and not much superstructure on top. Remove the bridge, convert the holds, add a flight deck and an island and you've got a carrier."

"Guess that makes sense."

"Janie and I kept in touch through the mail. After finishing up off the African coast the Santee operated out of Norfolk, Virginia for a while. I snuck home on a weekend pass and we got married. She was Catholic, I was Protestant and the church had strict rules back then. We couldn't get married inside so they performed the ceremony outside on the front steps. No pictures, no elaborate celebration … we even had to grab a passing pedestrian to serve as a witness. Our honeymoon was an overnight stay at her mom's house before we headed back to Norfolk. We rented an apartment and stayed there until I was transferred to the Pacific to serve onboard the Cabot."

"A whirlwind weekend," I noted.

"It was," Don replied. "But we had each other. A guy doesn't need more than that. I must admit, however, that marriage did present its share of complications. Seems I was always getting in trouble." He grinned and shifted his eyes toward Jan.

I took the bait. "How so?"

# The Perpetual Order of Old People

He reached into the folder and pulled out another picture. "Here's one of my favorites," he said, holding it up for Jan to see first. She glanced at the photo and blushed. "You're not going to show him that, are you?"

Don proudly turned the evidence toward me. It showed a group of sailors standing in formation, three rows deep. All but one wore their dress blues; the exception was a tall lad in the middle row who was dressed in white.

"Who do you think that poor guy there in his dress whites might be?" he asked. His expression suggested amusement mixed with a touch of embarrassment.

"I'm guessing that must be you," I replied.

"We were told to report to the tarmac in our dress blues the next day for a division photo. When I got home that night I learned that, during my previous deployment, Janie had tailored my blues to fit her, turned them into a very nice suit of sorts." He looked at his wife and beamed.

"Well, you never wore them," she said. "And I needed something." Then she winked. "And you did say they looked nice on me."

"They certainly did," he admitted.

He turned back to me and raised his eyebrows. "And then there was the issue of her showing up every time we returned to port. Ship movements were classified and no one was supposed to know our schedule but somehow my wonderful wife just had this feeling. We would pull in and she would be standing on the dock waving. I got more than one dressing-down for that but all I could say was that she had a newlywed's intuition."

"That's what happens when two people are meant to be together," Jan added. "You just know, you just get this feeling. Don didn't have to tell me when he was coming back … I'd just wake up knowing that today would be the day."

"No secrets between you two then I suppose."

Don took his wife's hand and their fingers entwined. "No need for secrets … and I wouldn't want any. The best thing about marriage is knowing there is someone you can talk to any time, about anything, and knowing that person will completely understand. I can't imagine going through life without that blessing."

## Chapter 11

When I returned home there was a message waiting on my answering machine. I hesitated, concerned that it might be Molly delivering more instructions or the real-estate agent asking for more concessions, before hitting the button.

*"Hi, it's Connie. Your machine's still working so I'm guessing you're still around. I was wondering if you'd like to continue our discussion from last week, over dinner perhaps. Might give us a chance to catch up. Call me."*

Dinner was at the Villa Maria, one of our favorite haunts when Connie and I were an item. Its location – roughly half-way between our respective homes – made it a convenient place to meet. The hostess led us to a small table in a quiet corner near the fireplace. She took our drink order and lit a candle on the center of the table before departing.

"I know I said this earlier," I began, "but I'm really happy you called."

"Me too," she replied. "Figured we deserved more than just a rushed lunch." And then she smiled. Connie could select from a grand palette of smiles: glowing when you agreed with her, bashful when you paid her a compliment, even melancholy when she could not change your mind. But the best smile, the real one, the one she did not need to paint on she saved for me. It said

*'I accept you, I appreciate you, life's rewards can be ours if we share them.'* That simple, soft, genuine smile danced on her lips and reflected in her eyes, captivating and lifting me, telling me there was one and only one right path into the future and that was whichever path we took together.

"So … how's the move coming along?"

The unenthusiastic tone of her question caught my attention as if she didn't want to hear the answer. I shrugged. "Frankly? I'm having trouble getting excited about it and that's spilling over into my packing schedule. I pick up an item but can't decide whether to keep or toss it and so I put it back and move on to the next item."

I laughed at myself then. "Last night I spent twenty minutes staring at my office desk phone. I made a lot of calls from that phone, sealed a lot of deals but that's part of the past now. Not likely I'll ever use that phone again and yet I can't bring myself to get rid of it. Really? Who gets sentimental about a desk phone?"

I immediately regretted saying that. If I had been sentimental about Connie two years ago we could both be in a better place today.

"And what happens after the move?"

It was there again, a hint of finality in her voice, the subtle suggestion that leaving was not cause for celebration. "Don't know yet. I'm headed out there soon for an interview."

She sat up straight. "What … what interview?"

# The Perpetual Order of Old People

I felt bad for broaching the subject but now it was too late. "Molly thinks I may be the magic bullet her company needs. She arranged for an interview and has put together a list of retirement communities she wants me to check out. I'll probably be in escrow there before I set foot on the plane here." I tried to smile but it didn't quite make it to my lips.

Connie stared back. She placed her elbows on the table and rested her chin in her folded hands. "Okay, sounds like Molly is happy … but are *you* happy?"

The answer caught in my throat. "I don't know. I thought I was doing the right thing when I sold the business. The job simply became too much for one person. I considered bringing in someone to help, perhaps take over, but knew I couldn't do the work I had already signed up for and train a replacement at the same time. So I approached an associate at another firm who I conferred with in the past and he made an offer to buy my business outright, basically buying my client list and having me set him up as their new service provider. To be honest I was floored with his offer – apparently, he saw more potential there than even I imagined. Dollar signs were floating around my head and I signed the papers, thinking I was unbelievably lucky and finally free to do anything I want."

That earned another smile from Connie. This one said '*you should have known better.*'

"But it didn't last, did it?"

I had no defense to fall back on. "Of course not. I miss being involved, having a purpose. That's why the idea of working for Molly's firm has a certain appeal. I don't know enough about the job but knowing one is out there – maybe waiting for me – is kind of exciting. But at the same time, I don't want to get dragged back into the rat-race. I hate to admit it but I've gotten a little lazy in my old age. I like knowing that I don't have to meet a deadline every day."

"You still argue both sides of the coin," Connie noted.

This time I chuckled. "And yet I always manage to lose the argument. To answer your question … no, I'm not happy. Moving is merely the lesser of two evils."

"I see," she replied. "And what is the greater evil?"

"Stagnation. Actually, it's not that bad … no … let me rephrase that. It's worse. I'm not getting younger and what you told me years ago is finally starting to make sense, that when I get old I'm going to want the permanence and support of family. Here I have nothing and … to be honest … I'm wary of what the future has in store. Out west I'll at least have a purpose and someone to come around when I can no longer get around by myself. But that still leaves me alone at night, an addendum to some other family but not one I can call my own. Never thought I'd be afraid of being alone but now that I know what it's like … it's terrifying."

I copied her pose: elbows on the table and hands folded. "You were so right. As soon as I let go of my career there was nothing. Nothing but a big gaping hole in my life and a big, empty house that I don't want to come home to."

This was not how I wanted to spend the evening but it felt good to let this out, good to know that Connie was hearing this. I think she understood how I felt.

"If I make this move I'll have a new job to distract me and occasional visitors but it still leaves that gaping hole. That one I can't run away from."

"You need someone to fill that hole," she told me. "Someone to share your meals and walks and nights and … and your future with. Life was meant to be shared, Jack, to be witnessed and appreciated by others. It would be a shame not to have that opportunity."

I nodded agreement while my mind backtracked through the recent past. "That's what Doc advised. Do things together."

"Doc?"

It took a second for me to catch up. "Friend of mine. Actually one of several new friends, war vets mostly, who meet for coffee in the mall. They've sort of adopted me."

"So you're not alone now," Connie noted.

"Not for an hour or so each day … but my nights are pretty pathetic." It sounded more depressing than I intended but it summed up how I felt.

She waited for me to look into her eyes again. "You said '*if.*'"

Her statement confused me. "What?"

"You said '*If I make this move,*' as if you haven't fully committed to the idea. Are you still on the fence?"

No doubt she knew the answer and was merely forcing me to face the question. "I suppose. I see the pieces falling in place but, subconsciously, I think I'm hoping for a stay of execution ... for the job to pass on me as a candidate or for Molly to come back with the news that she can't find any acceptable housing in the area. I don't expect either of those to happen though."

"Don't do this if you're not sure, Jack." She paused then, perhaps to see how I would respond. I didn't.

"Do you want my take on the matter?" she then asked.

I nodded eagerly.

"I think you've boxed yourself in, convinced that you have only one choice, either lonely here or lonely there. Try thinking outside that box. Stay in touch with your niece and nephew but stay here where they can't dictate how you live your life. Then find yourself someone to live it with."

Had it not been for the darkened room she might have seen me blush. "Yeah, right. Who'll take a second look at this spring chicken?"

She smiled first, the way she used to smile for me, and then raised her eyebrows. "You and I hit it off pretty good once before. Maybe we could pick up where we left off."

# The Perpetual Order of Old People

It felt like someone jump-started my heart, forcing me upright in the chair. I played the scene over in my head to make sure I heard correctly.

"You and me? I … I thought you were seeing someone … and that it was serious."

Another smile, softer this time. "I always keep my options open in case a better deal comes along, one with more promise and potential. And … I might have embellished a bit when I said it was serious. I was still mad at you at the time."

The road ahead had taken an unexpected turn and I dared to follow her lead. "So you think I might be a better deal?"

She took a sip of wine but did not break eye contact. Then she folded her hands on the table. "Jack, my husband left me two years before you and I met. I was really hurt at first, then I was really mad, and finally, I agreed that he was right, it *was* for the better. Ours was a marriage of convenience, two up-and-coming corporate superstars who fit together like puzzle pieces. Except we were pieces from different puzzles. His picture did not complete mine, nor mine his. We could look at each other, and touch, and be proud that we fit together so perfectly and yet there was no connection between us, no spark, no chemistry. That's why I was so mad at you … we *had* that spark, the chemistry that melds two people into one. We each knew what the other wanted and wanted to be the one who made it happen. Only I wanted it for the long-term and you weren't ready yet."

Everything she said was true. I had been on a career high, not wanting to spoil the mood and so afraid of what a partnered-future might bring that I refused to look in that direction. Holding on to my freedom left me trapped but when she extended her hand to rescue me I pulled back. Her hand was there again.

"You really think we have a chance?" I asked. It was a foolish question … this night would not have happened if she didn't believe in miracles.

She leaned closer, close enough for the candle to illuminate every beautiful curve of her face. "I'm not saying there won't be challenges. There's ten years between us Jack and I'm not ready for retirement. My job is still immensely important to me and it takes up a great deal of my time, but it's not love. I know what it's like to be in love and I want that back. When the job is gone I still want the love. I think we still have the spark and I believe it can grow into something stronger, something permanent, but if my job is here and you move away then we'll never know for sure."

# The Perpetual Order of Old People

## Chapter 12

The morning brought snow – lots of it – but I fought my way to the mall. I needed to walk, to sort out my thoughts, to review the prior evening with an open mind and try to understand why I felt so conflicted. And I needed to talk. Emotions, concerns, and questions jostled in my head, none staying in focus long enough for serious consideration. I needed to filter them, draw them out for rational analysis through the process of communication but even Tom had been wise enough to sit out today. And so I walked the concourse, loop after loop, oblivious to my surroundings as I struggled with knowing that soon I'd be on a plane heading west with my future at stake and couldn't decide what or where I wanted that future to be.

Here there was Connie, and while that grand adventure came to a depressing end the last time around there were hints of hope among the embers that still glowed after last night's dinner. Would it work for the long term? Was there enough connection between us, enough to build on that two people might meld into one, to have and to hold until? Would we both be happy … her days spent in a boardroom and mine walking in circles while waiting for night to bring us together again? A part of me wanted to believe so, and a part feared it was fantasy. Would I be jealous of her continued contribution to some noble purpose, powering the wheels of commerce while I wear out the heels of my shoes? I could spend my days preparing elaborate meals and planning romantic dinners but would I be content being the cook while she brought home the bacon? The idea seemed chauvinistic and yet the thought of swapping roles chilled the air around me.

And what waited out west? Family for sure, though a part-time family at best unless Molly had plans to marry me off. Nights – most of them at least – would still be spent peering over a chessboard or partially completed vista of mountains or seascapes. Would there be malls to walk or stories to hear? It amazed me that I had accepted this move as my fate, as the lesser of evils, without thoroughly researching my options.

I was mid-thought when something up ahead caught my eye. Samurai was there again, the invincible warrior statue coming straight at me. I maintained course while looking to the side as if absorbed in a window display. After a few adjustments I had my stride right and was braced for the collision, my left foot planted firmly behind me at the moment he stepped into my lane. Our shoulders connected and this time I threw my weight forward. The impact spun him around and a second later he was sprawled on the floor. My shoulder hurt but I suspect not as much as his pride. He sat there leaning back on his hands, his mouth open and his eyes caught somewhere between angry and astonished. It was my first up-close look at him and, in retrospect, I'm surprised I managed to knock him off his feet. He was a bit shorter than me but solidly built, lean and muscular, and I can only attribute my victory in this round to his careless assumption that the outcome would be different.

"We need to talk," I said while extending my hand to help him up. He refused the offer and quickly returned to his feet.

"I have nothing to say to you," he replied. The anger was still there, in his eyes, in his voice, in the way he hunched forward as if bracing for another assault.

As the seconds dragged on I began to worry that the encounter would end in a stalemate. "I think you do, and I think you find it easier to hide behind whatever bug you've got up your ass than to face it head-on like a man. This is your chance. Let's talk."

When he didn't respond I tried a different approach. "Coffee?"

He continued to stare, his eyes narrow and focused, his breathing low and heavy like an inaudible growl. But he didn't turn away ... he continued to face me, man-to-man. Then, with no change to his expression, no sign of acceptance or compromise he said, "Tea."

Stripp Teas was exactly that, a narrow strip of retail space wedged between a cosmetics boutique and a nail salon on the lower level. I had walked past it countless times without looking inside and now regretted that oversight, as it was actually quite charming. The walls were lined with paintings, most of an oriental nature and denoting the benefits of relaxation. Placards described the history of various teas and alcoves held decorative tea pots and cups. A lone employee manned the counter along the back wall and above him, a menu listed the beverages available that day. Black and orange-pekoe – the only teas I knew by name – were not there so I motioned to Samurai that he should order first and then told the attendant I would have the same. Once served, we sat at one of two small tables pushed up against the side wall.

"Let's start with names," I said. "I'm Jack." I extended my hand but again he refused it, choosing instead to stare at me, his expression now more apprehensive than angry as if expecting a trap. As I went to speak again he answered, "Akio."

"Akio," I repeated. It didn't matter if it was a first name or last; it was a start.

"I gather you don't like those of us who sit each day in the food court. In fact, I was told you feel we don't belong there. Can you help me understand why?"

Another bout of silence followed but I waited, convinced that he would not have come this far if he didn't have something to say.

"You shouldn't be there," he finally said. "You shouldn't be sitting there, laughing about what you did to us. You should not be proud of what you did."

"Did to who?"

The question appeared to infuriate him. "The Japanese!"

It seemed obvious but I asked anyway. "During the war?"

# The Perpetual Order of Old People

"No! After the war, when you sent the occupation forces."

What little I knew about the post-war occupation of Japan by Allied forces would fit on a postage stamp but I tried, looking for something that might explain his bitterness. I came up empty.

"She was only sixteen years old," Akio continued. His eyes had changed, resentment giving way to despair.

"Who?"

He shook his head slowly. "Her father went to war and never returned. Her mother died when you bombed Tokyo. She was homeless. The occupying forces were told not to hurt the Japanese. Your MacArthur told his men not to hurt the Japanese but that didn't stop them. Those men were there to distribute food, to keep our people from starving but one of them held back. He wanted something in return, something he had no right to. She was only sixteen years old. What else could she do? Nine months later my father was born."

A part of me wanted to speak up, to fire back, defending Americans who had been thrust into a war they didn't want ... but a part of me knew that Akio wasn't finished and interrupting him now would only jeopardize the fragile line of communication we had established.

"She could have chosen to abort the child, many Japanese women caught in that situation did rather than live with the shame, but he was the only family she had. She raised him as best she could. My father grew up without honor, without pride. He worked hard, as hard as anyone, to build a life of his own but always lived under the shadow of disgrace. Only after many years of trying did he find a Japanese woman who would accept him as her husband. When I was born I too learned to live in shame. I was twenty years old when my father was transferred to America and now that I am here, now that I see how your war heroes sit around and laugh about what they have done, the anger that my father felt erupts inside me."

I let his words hang in the air, hoping some of that anger would dissipate with them. "War brings out the worst in people," I told him. "And no nationality is immune. A study of history, yours included, will confirm that. Atrocities occurred on both sides and what cruelties a young man might commit at a time of war would likely appall him later in life. Our perspective regarding other people, friend or foe, changes as we get older, just as nations who are enemies during one generation become allies the next. I'll tell you this much, however … those men sitting at the table upstairs aren't gloating. They have seen the downside of war and have to live with the scars. Many of them are from around here, they grew up here, they were friends before the war and they get together now to support each other. For some of them, each other is all they have. Our nations are no longer at war and those men are not your enemy. You have no reason to believe me but neither do you have just cause to condemn them. The war you are fighting now exists entirely within you and I hope you can find some way to call a truce. It would be a shame to become a casualty of your own life. Trust me on that ... I know. I've been there."

Several long seconds passed as we studied each other, our eyes locked, our expressions impassive. In time he pushed away from the table, then turned without speaking and left the shop.

Neither of us had touched our tea. I tried mine; it was tepid but tasty. I would have ordered another if I knew what it was.

# Chapter 13

There was an air of playfulness around the group table the next day. Everyone had a story to tell about the monstrous snow piles they removed from their front steps, or their intrepid trip to the mailbox to fetch the paper, or in Doc's case the snowplow operator who gracefully removed the picket fence bordering the rose garden while clearing the driveway. These men are survivors; they faced the elements and lived to gripe about it.

The morning progressed with innocent anecdotes, updates on children and grandchildren, observations – favorable or otherwise – regarding the current political environment and repeated pleas that someone eat the last donut from a box of pastries left on the table. At one point Harris rolled his paper napkin into a ball and tossed it free-throw style across the table to Dent's empty coffee cup. It bounced off the rim and rolled to the side as some spectators cheered and others booed. "Close but no cigar," Harris lamented.

"Close only applies in horseshoes and hand grenades," Dent replied. "Want to try again?"

"Tanks but no tanks," was his answer.

"You want tanks? *I'll* give you tanks!" Dent ripped a small portion from the napkin, rolled it into a ball the size of a pea and placed it on the table. Then he cupped his right hand and placed it fingers-down on the table directly behind his ad hoc projectile. Harris accepted the challenge by laying his closed fist on the table across the way. With a flick of his finger, Dent sent the ball flying. It missed Harris's tank by several inches and the crowd jeered from the sidelines. Harris returned fire with equally dismal results. The battle continued, with the paper projectile flying back and forth until Dent picked up the ball and threw it down hard on Harris's hand, scoring a direct hit. His fists went up in triumph.

Harris's flattened hand now limped back in retreat. "Help me! Help me!" he cried out in jest.

"I win!" came Dent's victorious response.

"Yeah, but not a fair win," Harris complained, though it was clear from the other faces around the table that the battle was over and it was time to move on.

"All's fair in love and war," Dent proclaimed.

It happened in an instant. I saw it, as did others sitting nearby. Gus shuddered violently in his chair, his shoulders hunched and both hands clenched tight as if preparing for battle. "That ain't funny!" he yelled. "It ain't funny and there's nothing fair about war!" He stood and planted both fists knuckles down on the table. "Ain't nothing fair about it!"

An uneasy quiet fell around us. The only sound was that of Gus breathing, deep and heavy through gritted teeth. A vein on his forehead bulged as he glared, his eyes sweeping from one offender to the next. When they settled on me I tried reaching out.

"Can you help us understand why?" I hoped that by keeping my voice low the question would be viewed as an opportunity rather than a challenge.

"You know, for a newcomer here you ask a lot of nosy questions!" he snapped.

I nodded, determined to keep my end of the conversation social. "Sometimes the right questions lead to important answers."

That only angered him more. "Well, my answers ain't none of your business!" He grabbed his hat off the table and stormed away, his limp exacerbated by haste. His departure left the rest of us in an uncomfortable position: guilty of having wronged a friend but not knowing what we did wrong.

"Should I go after him?" I wondered aloud.

"Best not," Doc advised. "I think he needs to be alone with his thoughts right now."

I considered that for a moment. Something Gus said troubled me as if I was personally responsible for offending him. My mind raced through the conversation but the words were just noise in the background; my focus was on the finger of blame pointing back at me.

"Actually … so do I."

I stood, nodded farewell to the table and left.

One advantage to a long, solitary walk is the opportunity for self-reflection, a chance to dissect our faults and weaknesses, laying them bare and analyzing the roots of our individual evils in the hope of understanding why and where we fall short. Hearing criticism from others, even well-intentioned constructive criticism triggers a natural defense mechanism that questions the validity of the message but the message is loud and clear when you hear it from yourself and what I heard now troubled me.

*Nosy?* No one has ever accused me of that before. Sure, I ask questions but questions are the tools of the consulting trade, the basis of learning and the building blocks of understanding. To be inquisitive demonstrates an interest in someone and any questions about them should be viewed as a compliment, a sign that their life is important enough to be shared. To that end, I have always seen myself as a catalyst in elevating a person's opinion of himself. Molly, on the other hand, is the nosy one, always curious, always snooping for specifics, digging deeper into private lives. Is that how others see me? Are my attempts to get to the heart of the matter viewed as intrusive? Maybe I'm going about it wrong. Maybe I've picked up some bad habits from Molly. They say that insanity is inherited – you get it from your children. Maybe I've inherited Molly's propensity for prying. If so then how do I change my approach? How do I get others to see me as caring, considerate, compassionate me and not meddlesome Molly? How do I fix this?

Good question.

\* \* \* \* \*

# Jeff Russell

When morning arrived I returned to the scene of the crime, still uncertain how I would react if confronted again by Gus. I spotted him standing at the far side of the food court, coffee in hand, but couldn't tell if he was waiting for everyone to show up at our table or debating whether to join us. In time he wandered over. The chit-chat died down as he took his seat. Several people offered a 'Good Morning' but those greetings were ignored.

"I have it on the highest authority," he began, "that I owe you all an apology ... and maybe an explanation for my behavior yesterday." He looked at each of us in turn. "This won't be easy for me so don't expect an encore."

He picked up his coffee but hesitated and placed it back on the table. Then he cleared his throat. His hands were folded before him and his eyes were fixed on the coffee cup but his focus appeared to be somewhere in the past.

"I was commander of an M4 Sherman during the North Africa Campaign. We were on a scouting mission and had just cleared the crest of a small hill when I spotted what looked like a Panzer in the distance. I was sitting in the turret seat and yelled to my driver, Bobby Ingalls, to stop. As I leaned down to fetch my binoculars I caught a glimpse of a muzzle flash and ducked below the edge of the hatch. An instant later something blew away the front of our tank. Bobby died, along with Jim

Healy, my machine gunner. They were both good kids. We ran a lot of patrols together."

He closed his eyes, perhaps debating whether to go on, or perhaps saying a prayer. Then he came back to us.

"The tank was dead but we still had control of the turret so I yelled to Brett Ambert, my gunner, to aim in the direction of the flash. He yelled something back but I couldn't hear him – both my eardrums had burst in the initial blast. It was crazy, I suppose, but we were a sitting duck and a second shot would have finished us off. I kept loading shells into the breach and Brett kept firing until we saw an explosion and a lot of black smoke. Figured we'd hit whatever took us out. Wasn't until then that I realized a chunk of my calf was gone."

Gus wrapped one hand around his coffee cup but left it there, resting on the table. "There was smoke everywhere inside, acrid choking smoke and I knew we had to get out. I pulled at Brett but he fought me, motioning for me to go. I think he wanted me to leave him there but I couldn't do that. I stood on the turret seat and pulled him by the shoulders. Finally, he reached up for a handhold and together we got him out the hatch. That's when I saw it; both legs blown off below the knee. I used our belts to make tourniquets but it was too late, he'd lost too much blood. All that time I spent firing shells might have saved my life but it cost him his. He died before help arrived."

No one spoke as Gus scanned the faces around the table. He stopped at Dent. "You said all's fair in war. It ain't. Nothin fair about it. I was in charge of that tank, I should have died with my crew. If I had come over that hill cautiously we might have seen the danger and had a chance to back up before getting blasted. Bobby and Jim went without having to think about dying. Brett had time but I think he knew it wouldn't be long. I've thought about their deaths for sixty years now, wondering why, wondering how they would have turned out if they survived instead of me. Who would their families be? Who would they drink coffee with every morning? Who would they go home to at night? Why should I have this good life and they don't?"

His head dipped and then swayed from side to side. "It just ain't fair."

Finally, he slumped back and folded his hands in his lap, remaining that way for some time before leaning forward again to sip his coffee. "So that's my sad story. Any questions?" At that point, he turned to me as if asking nosy questions was my job. The look on his face was unmistakable; he was daring me to ask for more when he had already given all.

"Just one," I replied. "Who was the higher authority?"

He shrugged and a thin smile escaped to his lips. "Who else … Emma."

A quiet settled over our table, the reverent quiet that follows the baring of a soul and the peace of having a great load lifted. I looked across at a fellow named Gus that I didn't recognize. This Gus appeared relieved,

# The Perpetual Order of Old People

liberated, perhaps even open to the public. His eyes looked tired but inviting, and that thin crest of a smile was still there. The tranquility of the moment was shattered by a woman's cry from across the court.

"Help! Please help!"

Doc sprang out of his chair. It seemed a reflex movement, instinctive and ingrained, and in the time it took the rest of us to realize that something was terribly wrong Doc was already headed through the crowd. With strides faster and longer than I could manage he reached a table surrounded by on-lookers. I caught up to him and stood out of the way, unsure of the mission but ready to assist.

In the center of the gathering, a middle-aged man sat gripping the table, his face an alarming shade of blue. A woman sat beside him, sobbing wildly, her hands clutching his and her own face etched in fear while a young man slapped desperately on the older man's back. I turned to Doc and a scene flashed through my mind, that of a young medic with inadequate resources and insufficient training standing over the mangled wreck of a fellow soldier, wishing he wasn't the one who made the difference between life and death. Doc swallowed hard and drew in a deep breath.

"Make a hole, people!" he bellowed.

I hadn't heard that command in years and was certain few of those watching had heard it before but apparently, they got the message. The crowd parted as Doc stepped forward. He knelt down, grabbed the man by the shoulders and shook him to get his attention. "Are you choking?"

The man nodded in quick, anxious bursts and pointed to his throat. His eyes were opened wide, too wide, as if they were bursting out of his head.

"On your feet!"

The poor man was barely out of his chair when Doc came around behind him. He wrapped both arms around his torso, just below the ribcage, balled one fist, grabbed that with his free hand and yanked upwards so hard that it lifted the man off his feet. He did this a second time and then a third before the man's head fell forward and he coughed something the size of a meatball onto the table. A sucking sound that was half panic and half relief followed. Doc lowered him into his seat, then came around front to face him. Once again he went down on one knee.

"Breathe. Deep and slow. I want to hear you inhale."

Several breaths later the man was able to look at Doc and nod. His eyes no longer bulged but they pleaded for reassurance.

"What's your name?" Doc asked. The question was casual as if the worst was over and all that mattered was a friendly introduction. My heart was still pounding, my face still flushed from the rush of adrenaline but Doc appeared at ease.

"Eduardo." The response was cautious, barely audible as if he was afraid to speak aloud. He wiped the back of his hand across a thick, graying mustache.

# The Perpetual Order of Old People

A bottled water sat on the table. Doc appropriated it, twisted off the cap and handed it over. "Okay Eduardo, small sips, slowly. Show me you can swallow."

Eduardo complied and after three sips managed to speak. "I'm okay. I'm okay." He raised his hand again and wrapped it loosely around his neck. "It hurts."

It was only then that Doc volunteered a smile. "You'll survive."

Eduardo took another breath and let it escape as the color returned to his face. "Thank-you."

Doc looked unusually tired. His head dipped slightly and his eyebrows appeared weighed down by grave responsibility. Yet there was a hint of relief in his smile. I wondered how it must feel, whether saving a life could, in some small way, help erase the memories of all those he could not save. He stood and patted Eduardo on the shoulder. "I'll be sitting right over there," he said, pointing back to our group. "You stay here where I can see you. Any problems, just wave. Remain seated for at least twenty minutes before you try walking."

"I will. Thank you again."

The woman who had been sitting at the table with him came around to hug Doc, the trickle of tears still on her face, while the young man attempted to shake his hand.

An amazing thing happened at that moment – the tension that gripped everyone, participant and spectator alike, evaporated like fog in the morning sun. The show was over. Life marches on.

My pulse hadn't yet slowed to normal when we turned and came face to face with Akio. He stood there, silent and motionless, his eyes fixed firmly on Doc. Then, once again, something amazing happened. He put his hands together and started to clap, slowly at first but then more rapid. Others joined in and soon applause came from all around us. Doc seemed not to notice, his full attention was on Akio. When the clapping faded away Akio placed his hands at his sides and bowed from the waist, a slow, respectful gesture. After he straightened up he said something in a language I did not recognize. Doc smiled and nodded gratefully. Maybe he understood Japanese, or maybe he simply understood that a truce had been declared. With that Akio turned and walked away.

"Good job, Doc," Harris said as we returned to our seats. The words were spoken quietly, with admiration, and others around the table nodded in agreement. I still trembled inside but they appeared to take it in stride. It left me wondering if this was not the first time they had seen Doc in action.

# The Perpetual Order of Old People

## Chapter 14

I'd forgotten how much I dislike flying. Years ago it was simple: show up, buy a ticket and hop on a plane. Free carry-on baggage, free meal, and a movie. I never watched the movie – my head was always buried in a business proposal or shipping document – but it was nice knowing that the airline cared enough to woo me with an abundance of amenities. Sadly those days are gone. At least the hours passed quickly as I read through everything Molly sent me and what little I found on-line regarding Cabern Ventures. By the time we touched down, I was convinced that my background would more than suffice when dealing with any problems they faced.

The ride from the airport to their corporate headquarters seemed unusually long. I had been to the desert southwest before to meet with clients and back then the vast stretches of land separating airports, business centers, hotels, and residential neighborhoods merely provided additional time to rehearse my presentation or focus on a specific business-related dilemma. Scenery went past unnoticed, traffic jams were a petty inconvenience and the frustration I read on the faces of other drivers was their problem, not mine.

This trip was different. I drove from point A to point B while considering the possibility of taking up permanent residence in the wild, wild West. Was I prepared to deal with hours of unproductive time spent behind the wheel or of having to walk indoors during the summer months because it's too hot outside? I also felt something I hadn't in the past – homesickness. Living in the Northeast put all my favorite places – Cape Cod, Boston, New York City and the mountains of Vermont – just a few hours away by car. Living here meant finding new favorite places and needing either an aircraft or stagecoach to get there.

Despite the apprehension preceding my arrival, I felt like my old self again – business suit, leather portfolio, professionally confident – as I stepped into the lobby at Cabern Ventures. It was about what I expected: small, neat and modestly decorated. Given their non-profit status and the fact that most customer interaction takes place over the phone there is little point in trying to make a great first impression at the front door. The receptionist's eyes went wide when I told her my name.

"Oh! Good morning, Mr. Brouder. Please come with me. Mr. Tillerman is expecting you." She had an exuberant bounce to her step as she led me down a mahogany-paneled hallway. A brass placard that read *Charles Tillerman - President* marked our destination and she knocked on the doorframe.

"Mr. Tillerman? Mr. Brouder is here to see you."

An older gentleman looked up from behind a massive desk. My first impression placed him in his late-eighties but I shaved off a decade when he stood and hurried across the room. He was shaking my hand even before he came to a stop.

# The Perpetual Order of Old People

"Good morning! I'm Chuck Tillerman. Thanks for coming." He directed me to a chair across from his desk and then sat down again. "How was your flight?"

"Uneventful," I replied. "Which is the best kind."

"Excellent! Can I get you a coffee?"

"No, thank you. I've reached my limit for today and it's …" I glanced at my watch. "Not even 10 AM … your time."

He settled back into his chair. "Fine then. First off, we appreciate your making the trip out here. I realize it must have been an inconvenience, especially coming after retirement, so on behalf of the board of directors, our deepest thanks."

It was the most heartfelt welcome I could recall and I nodded, grateful but somewhat perplexed. Seldom had I met with a corporate president and never – to my recollection – had the board of directors been aware of my services, pending or otherwise. Regardless, I wanted to appear as the cool, calm professional who is equally at home on the loading dock and in the boardroom. "It's certainly my pleasure," I told him.

Tillerman leaned forward and folded his hands on his desk. "Let's get down to business. Molly has told us a great deal about you. She's really wonderful and we're delighted to have her here. She thinks you're pretty wonderful too, and based on your resume and credentials the board tends to agree. Cabern Ventures fulfills a real purpose in the secondary education field and we want to see that continue and grow. We want our reach to touch every community that is struggling to educate the leaders of tomorrow. To do that we need the right man standing watch as the OOD."

He followed that with a playful grin. "Did I get it right? You stood watch as the Officer of the Deck onboard a submarine?"

I responded with an awkward stare while considering his question. "Um … yes, but … I'm confused. You're looking for logistics help, correct? That's my area of expertise."

He smiled then. "Yes, yes, we're aware of that and we're very impressed with your achievements. Some of them have a direct correlation to issues we face every day. But you have other qualifications that we desperately need – leadership experience, vision, the willingness to take on challenges and the drive to see projects through to completion. It is rare to find all those qualities rolled up in a single individual and that's why we want you on our team. And not just *on* the team … we want you leading it."

I shook my head, still not getting his point.

Tillerman settled back and patted the arms of his chair. "I'm moving on and we need someone to fill this seat. We believe you may be that someone."

My mind went blank, all except for the portion focusing on that massive oak desk.

We talked until noon, covering a wide range of operational matters, and then adjourned to a local

# The Perpetual Order of Old People

restaurant for lunch with other members of the executive staff. Introductions, questions, and answers flew back and forth over drinks, entrées and dessert. It was more food than I typically consume in an entire day and more tech-talk than I've engaged in for the past year but it felt good … really good. I was on top of my game, even after time off, and they were seeking my advice. This wasn't an interview … it was an invitation.

Our discussion continued back at the office. When Molly showed up to invite me to dinner at her place Tillerman announced that instead, I would be dining with the full board of directors. Molly was thrilled; I was still in shock.

Dinner took place at a club overlooking the eighteenth hole of a private golf course. When I confessed to never having played the game, several members of the board jested that I would love it and had plenty of time to learn. I accepted that swinging a club was part of the job description and let the matter drop. At least some amount of walking was involved in getting from tee to green.

Initially, the conversation focused on my background. It was clear they had seen my resume and I got the feeling they were testing me to see if I could support my claims. We quickly moved beyond that and began addressing hypothetical situations: how would I respond if this or that happened, what distinguishes a good deal from a bad one, how would I know when to add or cut staff. Some matters were beyond my scope of experience but no one appeared disappointed with my responses.

Things then turned serious, with the board expressing concern that finding a new president was their top priority and that no candidates from the executive staff appeared fit. At that point, I stepped into a familiar role, that of an outside consultant whose job was to ask critical questions and draw out relevant facts. I had met most of that staff earlier in the day and drew my own conclusions but wanted the board's opinion. Who were the key candidates? What were their responsibilities? How long had they been there? Where were they lacking? Most important, which of them might leave if an outsider stepped in to fill the opening and what would that loss mean to the company? This went on for over an hour, with me firing off questions and the board filling in the blanks.

"I feel like we're the ones being interviewed here," one member commented.

"My apologies," I replied. "Over the years I've found that while I don't always have all the right answers, sometimes it's enough to have all the right questions."

Tillerman was watching me closely. I could see the wheels turning in his head. "ARQ Solutions," he finally said. "A-R-Q ... all the right questions. Now it makes sense."

If anyone had made that connection in the past they never mentioned it, and as a result, his astute observation was deeply gratifying. "I've always been proud of that name," I replied. "It's a constant reminder that time spent looking for the right question is well invested."

"So what have the right questions taught you?" Tillerman asked.

I shifted in my seat, once again feeling the heat of the spotlight. "For starters, the right answers are almost always out there but not necessarily where you expect to find them. I've learned more about why things go wrong by talking directly to workers on the production floor than from their managers. And I've learned that often the biggest impediment to progress is human nature, the inherent resistance to change that springs from fear and uncertainty. Getting buy-in from stakeholders is easier if you address their concerns up front, if you ask for their opinion and recommendations, making them part of the decision process rather than trying to force change on them. But if I had to choose one lesson that was more important than any other it's that by talking things out, by asking questions and getting as much input as possible from as many players as possible, you sometimes discover that some great ideas aren't so great after all. Canceling a proposed program is always less costly than scrapping one that has already started and failed."

I thought a bit longer, wondering if the lessons of the recent past outweighed everything that came before. At this point in my life, I concluded they did.

"And on a personal note, Tom taught me that extending a hand can change a life, that a simple invitation to sit and talk can lead to insight and answers that might otherwise have gone overlooked. Doc taught me that the future is not dictated by the past and that we can't let previous failures keep us from trying again. John helped me see that, even when we have done great things, the credit for our accomplishments should go to those who inspire us. Will showed me that we are shaped by the way we respond to challenges and that facing our fears, day after day, can give us something to look back on with pride. Vic taught me to take a chance, to follow my instinct because great treasures are sometimes found in unexpected places. Thanks to Don I now realize that by living alone I've missed out on the best part of life and that burdens are easier to bear and good times are more rewarding when you share them. Mac taught me that, even with a lifetime of difficult memories, a sense of humor can help keep things in perspective. And Gus ... Gus taught me not to judge people; that even a grumpy old man – especially one who has become a prisoner of his own past – can end up being a hero with a heart."

The words came out on their own, spoken more to me than to the others present. "I've spent most of my life as that prisoner, happily safe in my little cage, content because I didn't know what it looked like on the outside. Now I know, and it's a little scary, but these lessons were a long time coming and I don't intend to waste them."

It wasn't much of a smile – more of a self-deprecating, what-the-hell, '*that probably sounded foolish*' smile – but it slipped out and I didn't care. Mac would have been proud.

The board sat there quietly. One by one they looked at each other.

"Friends of yours?" Tillerman finally asked.

I nodded. "The best kind, the kind that come together to lean on each other."

It was late when I called Molly from my hotel room. "Sorry we couldn't get together today," I told her. "This whole thing took off in a direction I hadn't anticipated."

"I'm so happy for you!" she replied without asking for details. A part of me wondered if she knew about this already and withheld critical information out of fear I might not make the trip … but by this hour the rest of me was too tired to care. We agreed to meet for breakfast the next day.

## Chapter 15

Molly arrived dressed in a grey skirt that ended just above the knees and a soft peach blouse worn open to reveal a silver necklace with a heart-shaped charm. It was a big step up from business-casual. My first impression was that she was hoping for another opportunity to rub elbows with the executive staff on my behalf today. Then I took a second look. Simply put, she was lovely, and I realized that where I had always seen a spunky little schemer who constantly went out of her way to help other people, those people likely saw her as an attractive, capable and caring young woman. I was busy chastising myself for that oversight when the hostess arrived and showed us to our table. A waitress appeared moments later and took our order.

"So, what do you think?" Molly asked. The excitement I heard on the phone last night was still there and when I gave her a playfully suspicious eye she grinned.

"To be honest, I'm not sure what to think. Obviously, I wasn't prepared for this. On the one hand I don't know enough about their business model to feel comfortable taking the reins, but on the other hand, I've talked to their staff and agree that promoting from within is not an option. Don't get me wrong – you've got good people there – but none of them have the level of professional exposure Cabern Ventures needs at this time. I've faced the challenges they talked about; I've been boxed into those tight corners and fought my way out."

"Well, I think you'd be perfect for the job," Molly replied.

I was shaking my head with uncertainty when our coffees arrived. The interruption gave me a chance to collect my thoughts.

"Perhaps ... except that I'm not sure I actually want the job. It has always been my opinion that the first qualification for being a manager is that you must *want* to be the manager. If you don't *want* the position, if a part of you doesn't ache to shoulder the responsibility and you don't value accountability over title and pay then you don't belong there. I've felt that want and chased that dream all throughout my military and professional career but retirement freed me from that burden and I must admit that being free feels pretty good. That said, a voice kept me awake most of last night, telling me the want was still there, that sitting behind the desk with my fingers on the pulse and looking for the next challenge to tackle would feel pretty good too. I hadn't expected retirement to be so dull."

The eagerness was still there in her eyes. "I know you feel that way, that retirement can be a two-edged sword for someone who has earned the right to take it easy but still wants to be involved. I've watched you all my life Uncle Jack. Yes, it's been from a distance but I admired you from that distance. You've been my role model. I've heard it in your voice, how passionate you get when you sign a new contract or come up with some brilliant fix that no one else could figure out and I believe that flame is still burning. You would have turned the job down already if it wasn't."

I sat there dumbfounded; my spunky little schemer had all the makings of a professional spin-doctor. First, she agreed with my reasons for not wanting the job and then she made the case that I wouldn't be happy unless I took it.

"You have a lot of your mom in you," I told her. "And you should be proud of that. If you admire anyone it should be her."

The words lodged in my throat but I managed to keep going. She deserved to hear it. "Did I ever tell you that she was the one who convinced me to apply for Officer Candidate School?"

Molly's jaw dropped slightly. "What?"

It was a revelation long overdue. "I had just finished my second year of college and was trying to decide what to do with my life. Guys were getting drafted for duty in Vietnam and I told your mom I was thinking of joining the Navy because it seemed like the safe way to get some real-world experience. When she asked me what I was going to do there I said I didn't have a clue. So she said to me, '*Listen, Jack, don't settle. If you can be captain of your track team and captain of the debate club then you can be captain of a ship someday. Don't settle for less than the best you can do.*' It was good advice, especially coming from someone so young at the time. I've used her little pep talk to keep pushing myself forward at every turning point since."

I sipped my coffee while reflecting on where those turning points had taken me. "If I've accomplished anything worthwhile then the credit goes to your mom. She was my inspiration. She still is."

By this time Molly's eyes were moist and mine were getting there. A change of subject was in order. "So … you knew all about this replacement thing beforehand, right?"

She responded with her trademark grin – half apologetic and half pleased. "Well … not exactly. We all knew that Chuck would be leaving soon and some of the staff, even a few of the board members were asking me questions about you, questions that had nothing to do with logistics. I put two and two together."

The urge to both compliment her for being clever and chide her for not tipping me off shifted to the back burner when breakfast arrived. I suspect she waited until I had my mouth full before she brought the conversation back to her agenda.

"There are some really nice houses out here. Most are an easy commute and a couple are located along a very pretty walking trail. I think you told me recently that you had taken up walking for exercise. Good for you! And I checked … not everyone who lives in a retirement community is actually retired."

She reached into her purse and pulled out a folded sheet of paper. "Here is a list of available places. Your rental car has a GPS so just plug in the address and you'll be all set. I'm out of work at five – call me then and we'll meet at Connor's place. He's hosting dinner tonight and we'll all be together for the big surprise."

My mind was still digesting the list of addresses when her last comment registered. I shuddered and looked back up. "What big surprise?"

She had her mother's smile ... and it was beautiful. "I promise you'll be back to your hotel before late and plenty rested for your flight home tomorrow." Then she took one last bite of her omelet, gave me a wink and hurried off to work.

Though I arrived hungry, I no longer had an appetite. The situation was rapidly spiraling out of control ... my control at least. The board wanted me in, the staff wanted me in, Molly wanted me in and I wasn't sure what I wanted. The job sounded ideal – plenty of challenge but less pressure than I'd faced in the past, plus a nice office and a competent staff to help make things happen. I sat there staring at a stack of pancakes that looked ominously like the career ladder I had labored so long to climb and I wondered if my brief retirement was nothing more than a breather before taking the last step. Could I do the job? Yes ... absolutely. But did I actually *want* the job?

Closing my eyes offered no escape. Instead, I heard Molly's voice in my head. "*We'll all be together for the big surprise.*" What surprise? Who else would be there? Was she fixing me up with someone from her office ...

# The Perpetual Order of Old People

some middle-aged foxy lady to keep me company when I wasn't tied up with work or family?

I studied the list of addresses, finished my coffee, left enough to cover the tab and tip and then got underway with my to-do list in hand.

## Chapter 16

Connor's place is a spacious ranch in a comfortably quaint neighborhood. Like most of the surrounding homes, it has a two car garage, neatly trimmed shrubs in front and a fenced-in backyard. The inside has likewise always impressed me – warm woodwork, sensible layout and plenty of space for a growing family. Given Tessa's constant whining about a lack of money it is comforting to know they aren't living in poverty.

I sat in the living room with their twins – Katie and Kyle – bouncing on my knees. My hands were wrapped securely around them as they playfully pushed each other to see who could knock who to the floor. I think I laughed as much as they did; it had been a long time since I laughed like that. Molly snapped a picture and I asked her to do the same with my cell phone, half-planning to show it around the group table when I returned. '*Uncle Jack with his family*' I would tell them … just before telling them goodbye. It was a scene painted in mixed emotions.

Despite my jovial expression and cheerful horsing around an undercurrent of anxiety flowed beneath the skin. I looked about to see who else might have slipped in, whether my blind date was now standing to the side, hidden behind the draperies and giving me the once-over. The rational part of me argued that I was being foolish, that I had no proof of a setup and that paranoia would spoil the evening and yet the rest of me kept

# The Perpetual Order of Old People

watch. I was absorbed in that dilemma when Connor took a seat next to me.

"Guys, why don't you give Uncle Jack a break. Go ask Mom if you can have a cookie."

Some things, apparently, are more important than bragging rights between siblings. The wrestling match ended in a tie and the twins scampered off.

"Mind if I pick your brain?" Connor asked.

I stretched the kink in my back and settled into the sofa. "Of course. What's up?"

"I have an opportunity for a promotion at work, a big one. It comes with a healthy pay raise but means a lot of travel and time away from home."

The concern in his eyes matched the anxiety in his voice. "Tess wants me to take it. She keeps pointing out how your career – with all the traveling and such – left you in good shape financially. I'm not so sure though. I like being home with my family." He took a glance back toward the kids. "Also, when my company offers someone a promotion they expect them to take it. Turning down an offer may mean you won't get another."

His eyes came back to meet mine. "Any suggestions?"

It was, perhaps, the greatest compliment I had ever received. Someone was asking my advice about a family matter, turning to me for guidance as a son might turn to his father. I savored the feeling for a few seconds before attempting a worthy response.

"I understand the money argument, and even more I understand the prestige. I took every promotion I could get, capitalized on every opportunity because it made me feel better about myself. But it was different for me; for me, the job was the goal, and a rather foolish goal at that. You have a family and for you, the job should simply be a means to some greater end on their behalf. I have come to realize – too late in life perhaps – that when the job goes away you still want your family to be there for you. My advice is to do whatever you must to be there for your family when they need you because someday you'll need them. If it means jeopardizing your job then so be it … there are other jobs out there. Just don't jeopardize the connection you have with the people you love."

I went to add something, to expound on the well-worn proverb that money doesn't buy happiness but my philosophical rambling was interrupted by the sound of the doorbell.

"I'd better get that," Connor said. "Thanks, Uncle Jack."

He didn't get far before Molly sprang from her seat and disappeared around a corner. A moment later there she was – foxy lady. Beautiful eyes, beautiful smile, slim with flowing golden hair and long, shapely legs extending from a short, tight skirt. I must confess to being intrigued; if this was Molly's idea of a blind date then my little spin-doctor also has a future as a match-maker.

# The Perpetual Order of Old People

Foxy stepped to the side and looked directly at me, perhaps because I was looking directly at her. Her impish smile and the twinkle in her eyes said *I know something you don't know*. Then she winked.

There was nothing I could do. I was a captive audience on an arranged date and it was only polite that I should stand and introduce myself. I tried but my legs held back, they refused to cooperate. I tried and failed again before a voice in my head said *she's not the one ... Connie is*. As I made one last attempt to get up Molly stepped in front of me. She was holding hands with a handsome young man.

"Uncle Jack, this is Ethan," Molly said by way of an introduction. "He and I are friends."

"Good friends," Ethan added, looking over at her. "Very good friends." When their eyes met Molly blushed; the color looked good on her. Then she turned back to me.

"I have a big favor to ask ... a really, really big favor."

I swallowed hard. My eyes darted quickly to Foxy, who was still looking at me, and then back again to Molly. "Is this the surprise you talked about?"

"Yes!"

Tessa's ears perked up and she drew closer, pulling Conner along to join her. Soon I was surrounded.

Molly trembled for a second and then held out her left hand to show me a beautiful diamond ring on her finger. "Uncle Jack … will you walk me down the aisle?"

On hearing that Tessa screamed with delight, an outburst that sent the twins running for cover. Connor laughed and gave Ethan a playful punch to the shoulder. I stood and said the only thing that came to mind. "Of course!"

Then Molly hugged me. There had been hugs in the past but none like this. This one locked me in an embrace that would be there long after she let go. This one dampened my shoulder with her tears. This one melted my heart. I closed my eyes and Connie's words came back to me. *I know what it's like to be in love.*

When I opened my eyes I saw Ethan standing just behind Molly, who still had her arms wrapped tightly around my neck. I extended my hand as best I could and he shook it vigorously. "I'm Jack, by the way. Uncle Jack, if you prefer."

"Great to meet you," he replied. "Molly talks about you all the time."

I smiled proudly. "I suppose she has your wedding completely mapped out by now."

Ethan grinned like someone sharing an inside joke. "She has it on a spreadsheet," he whispered.

Foxy stood behind Ethan and raised her hand in a quick wave. "Hi! I'm Ellen, Ethan's mom. He spilled the beans earlier but wanted me here for the announcement. My husband's working tonight, otherwise, he would have come too. I'm so happy to meet you!"

It was a strange feeling: relieved but maybe a little disappointed. "Pleasure's mine," I replied with a crooked smile and my head tilted off-center from Molly's continued grip.

When Molly finally let go she and Tessa hugged, and after they finished giggling and admiring the ring Tessa turned to me. "And now *I* have a really big favor to ask."

I waited nervously, wondering what could possibly top this night.

"We have the wine and all the fixings," Tessa continued, "but none of us has ever made chateaubriand. Would you do the honors?"

For a moment I had to fight back a tear of my own.


We sat shoulder to shoulder at the dining room table, arms reaching this way and that for a slice of beef or helping of veggies, everyone talking at once and happy to be there. It was a scene from a distant memory and it felt marvelous to be back again.

"So how long have you two known each other," I asked Ethan.

"Five years," he replied. "And we've been dating for three."

Molly took his hand and gave me a big smile. "We've been letting the flavors blend."

## Chapter 17

The flight back differed from any I had taken in recent memory. There were no contracts to review, no business plans spread over the tray table or spreadsheets on my laptop; only me, a window seat and a river passing by far below. The Missouri, I imagined – the great divide – with Molly, Connor and a new job on one side and the guys, the mall and Connie on the other. I've been forced to make difficult choices in the past but those always boiled down to a business decision; whichever option paid off better, faster or advanced my career farther was the winner. It's not the same when other people have a stake in the outcome, especially people that you've come to appreciate … and perhaps even love.

The nagging question of whether retirement had been a mistake never echoed louder in the canyons of my mind. What if I simply needed a breather? What if I was ready to get back in the game and finish what I started? If Cabern Ventures was indeed the final step up the ladder of success then it would be a shame not to take that step. Moving west offered the prospects of a new career and a chance to bond, really bond, with my family. No more boredom, no more worries about growing old and dying alone. Those entries looked pretty good on the balance sheet of life.

And yet something still didn't feel right. Something was missing in the loss column, some great negative that would balance out all the positives that kept telling me

# The Perpetual Order of Old People

to pack my bags. It didn't take long for the fog to clear; moving away meant leaving Connie behind. At one time losing her seemed destined but now it bordered on unacceptable. Why? I backed away once before and yet now I wanted to be a part of her life. Was it because the people who put everything on the line and made that commitment were happier than me? Was it because I would become the grumpy old man I saw in Gus if I didn't have a purpose to my existence, someone to dedicate myself to for better or for worse?

As always it boiled down to questions.

* * * * *

An eternity passed while I waited for Connie to get off work. We agreed to meet for drinks at a café in downtown Stamford, and based on the brevity of our call – I had promised to contact her as soon as my plane landed – I suspect she understood the reason. Her place, my place, and even the Villa held too many memories. It is easier to keep expectations in check when the future is not holding hands with the past. Arriving early gave me a chance to sit alone and consider what I was going to say, though the drink I had while contemplating the unthinkable did not help. She arrived on schedule, always her style, and I had her drink waiting alongside mine in a quiet corner booth where we could talk in private. A quick kiss on the cheek served as my welcome back.

"So how'd the interview go?"

It's always best to start with a neutral question, ideally one with a simple answer. I took a booster shot of cabernet before trying. "It wasn't the interview I expected. I went there with the understanding that their five-year plan hinged on some unique logistic challenges and that I might provide a solution. At most I figured a three-month assignment followed by a retainer agreement to patch holes and tweak the process. Not a serious job, per se, but certainly something I could handle without a lot of stress. At this point in my life, I'm not looking for stress."

"But it wasn't what you expected," she said.

I shook my head. "No, it wasn't. They're looking for a new president. That position will be vacant soon and they feel that my combined military and commercial experience makes me the ideal candidate."

I felt a little humble saying that … and a little afraid, mostly of how Connie would respond. Clearly, she noted my concern and kept me waiting. It was the second eternity I'd faced today and I wondered how many more would follow.

"Who are *they*?"

It was a fair question. "Everyone, to be frank. I met with the executive staff over and after lunch, then with the board during dinner. They're worried that they have no one to promote from within and I agree. All good people but none qualified to take the helm, not yet at least. So they started looking outside the box and found me."

"Why didn't you know about this beforehand?"

Rapid-fire strictly business questions, as is her style. "To be honest I don't know. Maybe they wanted to meet me first, see the person who would become the face of the company before saying anything. Or maybe making the offer was a last-minute decision. They may have been looking for a new president and also looking for some logistics help when someone put two and two together and decided that one person could wear both hats."

"And Molly never said anything about this? Surely she must have known."

My strictly business answers hit a roadblock when the discussion became personal and I became defensive. "I don't know that either. She may have known from the beginning that the job was bigger than she let on, or she may have learned that they were upping the offer while I was meeting with the board. In either case, she seems thrilled at the possibility."

"Are *you* thrilled?" If there were personal feelings behind her question they didn't show.

"No, I'm not."

My reply appeared to surprise her, which in turn made me feel a tiny bit in control. "I can do the job, and I admit to being seduced by the opportunity – it's a career plateau that I'd dreamt about for years – but it means continuing to pass on other things that I'm just now beginning to understand are important, things that I've gone without for my whole life and don't want to miss altogether."

I waited for her next rapid-fire question. It didn't come.

"Connie, the last time we talked you told me you knew what it was like to be in love. I got a taste of that recently. Molly is engaged … and she asked me to walk her down the aisle."

Connie's eyes opened wide. "Mischievous Molly is engaged?"

For the first time tonight I smiled. "Yes, and if I called her that in the past then I regret having done so. She's grown into a beautiful, talented and caring person and she's found a nice young man who recognizes those qualities in her. I'm very happy for both of them, and … and I'm honored that she asked me to do her this favor."

Connie laughed. There was a hint of sarcasm in it but it qualified as a laugh nonetheless and that took some of the edge off the evening. "You once compared walking down the aisle to walking off a gangplank. If I remember correctly you called it 'taking the final plunge' … or something like that." She gave me a sideways glanced and smirked. "Apparently you've changed."

I accepted her well-deserved barb with a gracious nod. "If I have then I owe that to you. You opened my eyes on these matters. Unfortunately, I'm a very slow learner and I'm sorry for that."

# The Perpetual Order of Old People

She let my mea culpa hang in the air. "So you've found a family."

The tide had turned and I saw a glimmer of hope for smooth sailing ahead. "In a manner of speaking. I had children sitting on my knees, young people gathered around me, and they even asked me to cook dinner – chateaubriand no less. Yeah … it was a family. I thought I'd given up serving a purpose when I retired but I found a whole new purpose being with them."

We'd been sitting across the table for some time and it was just now that our eyes met. Before then, I think, we were both worried about getting too close. I let the moment linger; some of our most poignant conversations in the past were left unspoken.

"I understand your dilemma," Connie finally said. "I know what it's like when your job becomes an extension of who you are. I'm as guilty of that as anyone. My job allows me to be in control and there's a wonderful sense of security in that. As long as I have my job I don't need anything or anyone else. But the truth is it doesn't work that way. I know what happens when the rest of your life abandons you. When my husband left me I sought shelter in my work, sought to prove that I still mattered, that I was still important and that was enough. Then I found you and started to believe again that there was more to life."

She went to say something, to elaborate I suppose, but stopped short.

"What I've learned," she went on, "is that there *is* more to life but it's shaky ground at best. If you want it then you have to work for it, and wait for it, and hope that the other person wants it just as much. And you must be prepared for the possibility that it might not work out. Most of all you must constantly remind yourself that the rewards at the end of the rainbow are worth the heartaches you may suffer while trying to get there."

She looked away, her beautiful features masked by the shadow of sadness. Both hands remained wrapped around the stem of her wine glass though she had yet to take a sip. In time she smiled bravely through tightly pressed lips and turned back to me.

"So … new job and new family. I suppose I should be happy for you."

I rocked my head slowly in small arcs. "But I'm not happy … not if you're missing from that picture."

Her eyes grew wide again and in them, I saw a teary glimmer.

"Let's talk about that," I said.

# The Perpetual Order of Old People

## Chapter 18

The interrogation that follows any extended absence from the daily routine is a universal ritual and for that reason, I'd spent the morning anticipating the questions and rehearsing how I would respond. *How was your trip?* Great! *What about the job?* More daunting than I expected. *Did they make an offer?* Probably a bit early for that. *How's the housing situation out there?* Got a glimpse but need to do more homework. *Did you see your family?* Yes! We had a wonderful time! *Will you be leaving us soon?* I didn't have an answer for that one.

I was prepared for the barrage when I approached the group table but those who noted my arrival merely nodded and turned their attention back to Doc. Tom spotted me and motioned toward the empty seat near him. I sat and leaned close.

"Gus is AWOL," Tom said quietly. "Didn't show up Tuesday and hasn't shown his face since. Not like him."

I listened in as Doc addressed the issue. "I'll call his house if he doesn't show up by the time we leave today, and if I can't reach him there then I'll check with Brookside. He confided with me that Emma hasn't been feeling well recently, that she's not in good health, and I think he's worried. Losing her will be very difficult for him."

He paused then, perhaps looking for the words or perhaps giving us time to accept the inevitable. Life marches on, sometimes without those we love.

Mac reached over and took Millie's hand. Eyes that normally overflowed with humor were now filled with a deep sadness. It may have been the thought of Gus losing Emma, or it may have been the fear of losing the love of his life, of having to go on when his whole reason for living cannot go on with him. I felt the heartache just by reading his face. It struck me odd that someone like me, someone who never allowed himself to get close enough to another individual to develop that kind of bond could begin to imagine how it must hurt when the bond is broken. For those who spend the better part of their lives in that type of relationship, navigating the ups and downs, bearing the trials and celebrating the triumphs, I'm sure the pain must be so much worse.

"On to other matters," Doc said. "A new coffee shop – appropriately named 'Thanks-a-Latte' – has opened across the way. They offer a senior discount so you might want to check them out. Also, I spoke with Akio, our friend formerly known as Samurai. He has accepted the position of assistant manager at a hibachi restaurant that is opening soon in Fairfield and has invited us to join in their pre-opening dress rehearsal taking place in a couple weeks. I'll get more details soon. Basically, they need a crowd of guests to give their greeters, cooks and wait-staff experience in dealing with a full house. Kate and I are attending and I hope all of you can make it as well. The meal is complimentary and I think our presence would mean a lot to him."

Harris snapped to attention. "Free food? I'm in!"

# The Perpetual Order of Old People

"We can always count on you," Doc replied. "And finally, Jack is back and I'm sure you all want to know about his trip so I'll turn the floor over to him."

I waved to acknowledge Doc's gracious introduction but was distracted by the sight of a young lady who had approached our table. She stood silently looking from one person to the next and soon all eyes were turned in her direction.

"Excuse me," she said, her voice barely audible. "I was sent to find someone named Doc. Am I in the right place?"

Her attire – an unbuttoned grey sweater, blue blouse, and navy skirt – was understated professional, which ruled out casual shopper and retail store manager. Both hands clutched her purse as she waited. In time Doc stood and extended his hand.

"I'm Carl Wilson," he replied, "but everyone here calls me Doc. Can I help you?"

She drew in a cautious breath, held it for a second and let it slip out. Then she smiled, an uneasy smile, the type that says *It's a pleasure to meet you but I wish I didn't have to be here,* before shaking his hand. "Hi. My name is Linda Fletcher. I'm from Brookside Health Care."

No one had to say it; it was written in sad eyes and downcast expressions around the table. Doc had been right. Not that anyone questioned his diagnosis but they are survivors and survivors remain hopeful until the battle is lost. Even Doc appeared shaken.

"Is this about Emma Waterford?" he asked. It wasn't so much a question as a request for confirmation.

Linda nodded. There was sorrow in her eyes, the gloom that follows the death of someone close, the breaking of a bond that had formed over many years.

Doc wrapped one hand in the other and bowed his head.

"She asked me to find you," Linda continued. "She wanted you to know that her husband, Gus, passed away two days ago."

What had, seconds before, been the quiet of sadness gave way to the silence of shock. There was no sound, neither from the table nor anywhere in the mall. There were no shoppers, no workers, no one beyond the solitude of our one, small table. It is the nature of shock; cutting off the outside world while the mind struggles to make sense of the incomprehensible. Not surprisingly, Doc was the first to recover.

"What happened?" he asked.

Linda appeared to relax as if the difficult part of her mission was over. "He was always there, visiting Emma, everyday … and when he didn't show up on Tuesday she became worried. We all did; we loved Gus. So we asked the police to do a well-person check. They found him in bed. We know he had heart problems but … well, we're still waiting for the coroner's report."

We sat there silently, absorbing and accepting. Death is a destination we all reach, though survivors prefer to hold on a little longer, extending the journey in the hope of one more adventure. That eternal optimism makes it harder for everyone when the journey comes to an end.

"Anyway," Linda continued, "Emma wanted you to know that Gus loved being a part of your group as much as he loved her. He'd come in every day and share your stories with her. His eyes would sparkle and she would giggle and then they'd both laugh like teenagers."

Linda bit her upper lip. "God, we'll miss his laugh."

She checked her watch. "I really must head back. I'm glad that I was able to find you, and I'm sorry to bring such sad news. It was nice meeting you." She looked around the table. "All of you."

As she turned to leave Doc called to her. "Please tell Emma that we are deeply saddened and that we will be up to visit her soon."

Linda smiled gratefully. "I will. Thank you."

No one spoke as we watched her disappear into the lunchtime crowd. The sounds of the food court – of patrons dining and children playing and shopper rushing past – slowly came back.

Tom sat straight up in his chair, placed his arms on the table and folded his hands. "Well people," he began. "Looks like we have a job to do. I can take Tuesdays and maybe Thursdays."

"I'll take Monday," Dent said.

"Put me down too," Harris added. "Whenever."

Apparently, they knew something I didn't. "What job are we talking about?" I asked.

"Visitor duty," Tom replied. "We'll pick up where Gus left off, visiting Emma. It's the least we can do."

I looked around the table at faces I had known for only a short while but knew better now than anyone I'd met in the past fifty years. They were soldiers who had lost one of their own, friends who had lost a comrade, a family who had lost a part of itself.

"Add me to the roster," I said. "Any day you need me."

Tom tilted his head slightly and squinted in my direction. "Thanks, Jack. We appreciate that. How much longer will you be around?"

Under the circumstances, I didn't feel much like smiling but one managed to slip through. "Indefinitely."

Once again the table fell silent.

"But what about your job? Aren't you moving out west?"

By now everyone was listening. "I turned down the job. They wanted me to take the helm, full time, but I convinced them that grooming one of their younger candidates made more sense. It occurred to me there was a reason I retired in the first place ... I needed to live for more than just a career. But I agreed to serve as a consultant working remotely. They have some serious logistics issues and that's my area of expertise so we struck a deal. I'll video conference twice a week, fly out to attend bi-monthly meetings and hang-out with the family while I'm there. Should be able to make everyone happy that way."

# The Perpetual Order of Old People

"Even Tessa?" Tom asked.

"They'll be in my will," I replied. "No problem there."

"And what about your house?" Doc asked. "Don't you close on it soon?"

I nodded. "I'll be bunking with Connie until we can find something smaller that suits our needs. Some nice townhouses have opened up by the lake, just a couple miles from here, and we're going to look at one this afternoon."

Doc gave me a sly look. "Connie? I don't recall you mentioning her in the past."

# Chapter 19

The entire group wanted to serve as pallbearers during the short walk from the hearse to the gravesite. Doc and I took the lead, port and starboard, while Harris and Dent did the same in the rear. The others traded on and off in the middle so that everyone had a chance to participate and no one became too winded. Lucky for us there were no hills involved. It was a brief but beautiful ceremony and we were proud to take part, piping Gus over the side as he transferred to his next duty station. Emma, surrounded by a small staff from Brookside, sat up-front in a wheelchair and fought back tears as she watched the love of her life ship out like so many times before. Then she smiled bravely, as if not wanting him to see her cry, and held her right hand up as if reaching out to touch his one last time.

A rifle salute split the air like the crack of thunder, serving notice to the heavens that a hero had fallen. A second followed and then a third. As the echoes faded, the soft refrain of a bugle joined in to bid its farewell. The honor guard then stepped forward to fold the flag, their solemn poise and precise movements expressing undying respect for one of their own. They paused mid-way through while a white-gloved sergeant tucked three shell casings into the crease of the flag. When the folding was complete he gently laid the tightly bound triangle on Emma's lap.

"On behalf of a grateful nation," he told her.

# The Perpetual Order of Old People

After the funeral we agreed to take a short break, getting some R&R before meeting at the mall the following Monday. When the time came I decided to walk there. Winter had released its grip and, amazingly, I felt invigorated. Perhaps it was the clear sky or the fresh air or the buds forming on the trees ... but whatever the reason I saw my life at the beginning of a new phase. It was a fascinating sensation, one based solely on outlook and yet that upbeat attitude found its way into my stride. As a result, I covered the distance at a young man's pace.

When I arrived at the food court Doc, Tom and several others were busy chatting away. In the middle of the group sat an empty chair, and on the table before it sat Gus's hat. The 'missing man' formation. I took my place among them and joined the conversation. Life goes on.

Later that afternoon I arrived at Brookside Health Care for my first appointed shift. I'd met Emma briefly during the funeral and told her how I looked forward to visiting with her but now the time had come and I felt a bit uneasy, not knowing what to expect. My trepidation began to fade during the short walk from the parking lot to the entrance, which could have been modeled after any of the nicer hotels I'd stayed at in the past. Decorative metal benches and ceramic planters lined both sides of a covered walkway that divided a small lawn enclosed by a nicely trimmed hedge. I could picture the scene in a month or two, with residents and visitors sitting on the benches and enjoying the fresh air, the blossoming flowers and the sound of children playing on the lawn.

Stepping inside reinforced the conclusion that my perception of health care facilities was sadly out of date. The foyer was warm and inviting, with couches and lounge chairs arranged in a small greeting area to the left. A table in the center offered a selection of magazines and the credenza against the wall held a coffee maker and complimentary bottled water. Straight ahead a young lady sitting behind an oak counter greeted me. She showed me where to sign in and then gave me directions to Emma's room.

The accommodations began to look more like a retirement home as I walked down the hallway in search of Room 127, yet again it was not what I expected. A large recreation room, with windows overlooking what appeared to be a garden, was filled with residents working on an arts and crafts project. In another room people sat in wheelchairs, theater style, watching a game show on a large screen TV. A bit further down the hall, a rambunctious crowd cheered an event of some form. Just as I paused to get a better look one of the many attendants traveling up and down the passageway asked if she could be of assistance. I gave her the room number and she beamed. "Oh sure, Emma! Straight down past the center island station, then third door on the right."

Emma was ready and waiting when I knocked on the doorframe. She sat in her wheelchair, hands folded on the blanket covering her lap. A curtain separated her side of the room from her roommate, who peeked around the divider, smiled and lifted a remote to turn down the volume on the TV facing her bed. "You sure are popular, Emma," she said. "Lots of handsome visitors."

The rest of her accommodations resembled private rooms I'd seen in upscale hospitals, with warm wood trim, individual closets, and cards, pictures and photos displayed on the walls and furniture. I had to cut my inspection short, however, because it was now show time.

"Hi, I'm Jack. You may not remember but we met …"

She looked up as I stepped closer and then waved me in. "Of course I remember you! You're the one who asks all the nosy questions!" Then she smiled, a beautiful, fun-loving smile no doubt prompted by the stunned look on my face. My mind raced back to review what I might have said or asked after the funeral, the one and only time we'd met before today. I didn't get far before she giggled.

"Gus told me all about you. And it's okay … you can ask me anything you like. But ask along the way, you're my date today and we're already late."

I sprung to attention and got behind the wheelchair. "Where are we going?"

"Today's Monday," she replied. "We're going bowling!"

Once again my face went blank. "All right," I said, somewhat perplexed as to how this was going to work, and started pushing her out the door. "Which way do we turn?"

"Left, then down the hall past the nurse's station, then past the offices to the first playroom on the right." Picturing my journey here in reverse allowed me to pinpoint our destination as the large room with the cheering spectators.

When we got there the crowd parted at the doorway. I positioned Emma alongside several other residents in wheelchairs and tried to make sense of what was taking place. Up ahead a petite woman in a wheelchair was about to release a plastic bowling ball. She brought her arm back and then swung forward, releasing the ball toward a triangle of oversized pins standing at the far end of the room. When it was over only the ten pin remained and once again the crowd cheered.

"That's Maddie," Emma said. "She's the league champ. I've got a dollar riding on her for the tournament."

When the match ended, Emma and I moved to the second-floor lunch room. Once again the setting was bright and cheerful, with handmade decorations, large windows separating the dining area from the hallway and equally large windows overlooking the great outdoors. I watched as meals were brought in on cafeteria trays, each earmarked for a specific resident and no doubt tailored to their dietary needs. I must admit that Emma's meal looked tastier than some of those served on board our sub when I was in charge of ordering the food.

We spent the remainder of our visit talking about the past: how she and Gus met, where I traveled while in the service, places we lived and so forth. When it came to the question of why I never married I paused. The answer was there but I'd never tried putting it into words.

"It wouldn't have been fair to either of us," I said. "Before retirement, I was dedicated to my job, but once you marry work should take a back seat and family should be priority one. At the time I couldn't see the benefit. That was my fault."

A moment of reflection followed. "But then I met Tom and Doc ... and Gus ... and all the other guys in the group and they opened my eyes. There's something greater out there, a reward that makes new titles and new contracts seem trivial in comparison. So now I have a chance to start over. I may have come to the game late but I'm young for my age and I believe there's still time."

"Well, don't look at me," Emma said with a playful grin. "You're not my type. And besides, I'm waiting for my next date with Gus … he promised to show me around his new place when I get there."

'*I'll love you forever.*' How many times had I heard that and brushed it off as sentimental nonsense? But what a nice thought …

# The Perpetual Order of Old People

## Chapter 20

### *January 2012*

In the five years since I joined the group the mall has changed in many ways: the centerpiece fountain is now a clear plastic globe that overflows with water and shimmers under multi-color lights, faux-leather armchairs have replaced the old wooden benches and – for better or worse – wifi-connected shoppers walk around bumping into walls, columns and each other while fiddling with their phones. Thankfully the food court is still the same. Connie and I arrived early today, pushed our tables together and waited for the others. As unofficial spokesman I wanted to be here when Chad arrived, which he did a few minutes later. He placed his Vietnam War hat on the table alongside his coffee, taking a seat across from me.

"So how long has this group been meeting?" he asked.

It took a moment to do the math. "Forever, I think. Maybe longer. The founding members were classmates back in the early forties who went to war, returned and started meeting to share stories and renew old friendships. You met a few of them yesterday, the others are either gone or have moved on. But the size of the group hasn't changed much. It's like the stores in the mall; out with the old and in with the new. Despite the attrition, we still manage to fill these two tables every day."

Dent arrived, followed shortly by Harris, Vic, Will, and John. By the time greetings were exchanged and everyone had a chance to reintroduce themselves to our newest member all seats were taken.

"It's a little nippy out today," Chad remarked.

Dent dipped his head to look over the rim of his glasses. "Nippy? Three below?"

Chad smiled as if he expected a reaction to his witty observation. "I come from North Dakota, remember? When my daughter talked me into moving out here I couldn't wait to experience your nice warm winters. Best move I ever made … that and bumping into you fellows. Expecting much snow today?"

"Nothing major … a dusting to a foot," Dent replied.

"Okay you two," I said. "Enough of that. Let's get down to business. First, I want to thank everyone for their generous contributions to the Gourmet-for-a-Day fund. Yesterday's class filled up quickly and the chicken cordon bleu was a big hit at the shelter. It's gratifying to see how many people there want to be part of the process, preparing the meal as well as sharing it. So please keep saving your coffee change … next time I promised them salmon almondine."

"Did you bring any leftovers for us?" Harris asked.

I could see that coming and shrugged. "The problem with great cooking is that there are no leftovers. Okay, next order of business. I want to take this opportunity to

# The Perpetual Order of Old People

officially welcome Chad into our little group. Chad, who has demonstrated his diligence, determination, and destitution by braving the elements two days in a row to be here with us should now be considered a member in good standing."

I raised my coffee cup, as did everyone else around the table. "Welcome, Chad!"

"Here-here!" someone said. "Atta boy Chad!" another offered. A "You'll be sorrrryyyy," came from the far end of the table.

Chad took it well, as well as anyone who becomes the butt of playful humor. "Thankyou-thankyou-thankyou," he replied. "I'm very glad to be here."

"We haven't talked about membership fees yet," I told him. "Everyone is expected to contribute stories from their past. Happy stories are always welcome, as are heroic endeavors and haphazard exploits. You, of course, will be required to sit through our recollections – stories we've all heard before but always enjoy hearing again. Every life is a story, every story is important and sharing our stories allows us to live on. The more people know about us the more we remain behind when our story comes to an end."

"Count me in," Chad replied. "One question to start … is it 'the group' or do you have a name?"

The others, cowards that they are, deferred to me.

"Indeed we do," I told him. "We are the Perpetual Order of Old People. The 'Old People' part, I believe, is self-explanatory. The 'Order' part implies that we are a society ... or at least most of the time we try to be social. And the 'Perpetual' part comes from people like you, new members who enter the fold and fill seats vacated by those who have transferred to new duty stations. With luck, this group will be here forever ... perhaps longer."

By this time Chad was giving me a funny look. "Wait a second," he said. "The Perpetual Order of Old People ... P-O-O-P ... Poop?"

Once again all eyes turned to me. I could hear Gus in the background ... *Say it! Say it!* ... but I chickened out.

"Let's not go there," I replied.

*The End*

# The Perpetual Order of Old People

Other books by Jeff Russell

*Cab's Lantern*
*Afterlight*
*The Dream Shelf*
*The Girl Who Watched Over Dreams*

About the author

I am a tale-spinner. My childhood heroes were Jules Verne and Victor Appleton II, architects of fantastic adventures. Hemingway stepped in when I discovered that the trials and triumphs of real people - those with limited physical and financial resources - are even more intriguing than science fiction. Today I follow that example with my characters. They are the 'you and me' of the world, ordinary people facing extraordinary circumstances, beaten down perhaps and yet determined to succeed. Invariably they find adventure, romance, and self-fulfillment, as should we all.

When not absorbed in the pages of some new author or hammering away at my latest manuscript I can be found living and running in Stowe, VT.

Learn more at www.CabsLantern.com

30511156R00100

Made in the USA
Columbia, SC
27 October 2018